# MASKED BY DANGER

## HUNTED MATES: BOOK TWO

## CHRISTA WICK

ONE LOST MATE...

# Contents

Previously published as *Alpha Curves* (c) 2014
by Christa Wick
Reissue & Editing by Evergreen Books Publishing
Proofreading by My Brother's Editor
Cover design by Violet Duke

# ALSO BY CHRISTA WICK

**Her Satisfaction** (*Rachel & Carter*)


DAMAGED HEARTS: LAST CHANCE ROMANCES

**Show Me How** (*Gunner & Willa*)

**Tell Me When** (*Dare & Eden*)

**Ask Me Why** (*Dante & Olivia*)


ENEMIES TO LOVERS STANDALONE

**His Curvy Temptation** (*Declan & Melanie*)


HIS TO CLAIM SERIES (*SMALL TOWN, BIG CRAZY FAMILY*)

Book 1: **Every Last Doubt** (*Adler & Sage*)

Book 2: **Every Last Touch** (*Walker & Ashley*)

Book 3: **Every Last Look** (*Barrett & Quinn*)

Book 4: **Every Last Secret** (*Sutton & Maddy*)

Book 5: **Every Last Reason** (*Emerson & Delia*)

Book 6: **Every Last Call** (*Gamble & Siobhan*)


UNTIL YOU SERIES (*CO-WRITTEN W/ TESSA WOOD*)

Book 1: **Unraveled** (*Corwin & Belle*)

Book 2: **Unveiled** (*Lucas & Theresa*)

Book 3: **Untapped** (*Teague & Charlie*)


MORE THAN A NIGHT SERIES (*CO-WRITTEN W/ TESSA WOOD*)

Book 1: **More Than a Friend** (*Noah & Patricia*)

Book 2: **More Than a Flirt** (*Jack & Ursula*)

Book 3: **More Than a Fling** (*Gary & Laney*)

[*each loaded w/ fan fave character crossover cameos!*]

---

PARANORMAL BOOKS

PROTECTED BY THE PACK SERIES (*MC SHIFTERS*)

Book 1: **Harboring His Mate** (*Taron & Onyx*)

Book 2: **Resisting His Mate** (*Braeden & Paisley*)

Book 3: **Enticing His Mate** (*Joshua & Clover*)

HUNTED MATES (*WOLVES & WITCHES*)

Book 1: **Mated by Fate** *(Two fated couples…)*

Book 2: **Masked by Danger** *(One lost mate…)*

Book 3: **Marked by Magic** *(Zero room for failure…)*

MYTHIC MATES (*VERY DIRTY PARANORMAL FANTASY*)

**Her Deviant Dragon**

**His Darkest Depths**

---

CHRISTA'S **DARKER,** *DIRTIER* SIDE

(WRITING AS C.M. WICK)

2-IN-1 ALPHAS AFTER DARK DEAL DUOS BUNDLE

**Hot Alpha Nights** (*Logan & Lily*)

**w/ Tempted By Trouble** (*Austin & Gina*)

SAVAGE TRUST SERIES (*INTENSE, LINE-CROSSING HEROES*)

Book 1: **Wrecked** (Luke & Marie)

Book 2: **Scarred** (Mikhael & Alina)

Book 3: **Frayed** (Trent & Daniella)

SAVAGE HOPE SPINOFF DUET (*BILLIONAIRE DOM SUSPENSE*)

Book 1: **His Trust** (Collin & Mia, Book 1)

Book 2: **Her Heart** (Collin & Mia, Book 2)

DANGEROUS PROTECTOR SERIES (*DARK & DEADLY ANTIHEROES*)

**Ruthless** (Callan & Avery)

**Her Only Choice** (Carson, Maddox, Regina)

**Dark Savior** (Dean & Garnet)

[*these are standalones in the same MC world*]

VOLATILE HEARTS: GRUFF & GUARDED BILLIONAIRE DOMS

**The Contract** (Beckett, Jace, Gabby)

**Seven Nights** (*Griffin & Katelyn*)

**The Billionaire Master** (*Jake & Alexa*)

2-IN-1 REVERSE HAREM/MENAGE DEAL DUOS BUNDLE

**Theirs to Keep** (Hunter, Daniel, Aldon, Casey)

**w/ Curve Negotiation** (*Maggie & Jack & Ryan*)

JOIN MY EMAIL LIST TO GET

NEW RELEASE & SALE ALERTS

PLUS SPECIAL FREEBIES / BONUS SCENES

# Book Description
## MASKED BY DANGER: HUNTED MATES (BOOK 2)

The **gruffest, most hardened** strike team leader in the wolf packs by far, brusque, brooding Cade Mercer has good reason for being so grouchy all the time. Unlike his men, he's already mated. To a strong, incredible, *button-pushing* she-wolf no less.

She was the one that got away. Literally. Iris North had rejected their mating and left the pack twelve years ago, taking his heart with her. For Cade, shifter biology isn't the reason he's stayed **a one-woman man** since. It's simply how he's built. Iris was it for him. And being alone for the rest of his life is a reality he accepted a long time ago.

*Until,* that is, he catches the scent of the newest latent he's ordered to extract. Not only is **the woman the furthest thing from a damsel in distress who needs saving**, she's a tough, big city homicide detective packing more heat than his men.

She also happens to be **his no-longer-missing mate.**

*Previously published in the Wolf Clan series (c) 2014, revised throughout with newly added content, extended story elements, and expanded world building.*

**The HUNTED MATES Series**

Mated by Fate *(Two fated couples…)*
Masked by Danger *(One lost mate…)*
Marked by Magic *(Zero room for failure…)*

# CHAPTER 1

Rain drizzled on Syracuse like a drunk pissing in an alley, the flow just enough to mute the city's other odors. With the passenger window down, Cade Mercer inhaled slowly, filling his lungs to capacity as his face grew wet.

Nostrils flaring and twitching, he searched for a scent unique among all the others to help him locate the mystery woman he and his team had been tasked to find. Detecting no supernatural presence, he rolled up the window.

Beyond gender, he had no clue what his team was out here searching for. The new leader of the Witches' Council had detected a strong, feminine signature loaded with magic. Those parameters meant the target could be a lone she-wolf or an orphaned female cub. Less likely was a woman with inactive shifter genes—a latent.

"Why do I feel like we are driving into a trap set by

Hunters?" his driver asked as they waited for a traffic light to turn green. "Like, we're gonna get there and it'll be one of those freaky-ass meat-sack things."

*Freaky-ass meat-sack thing* was a pretty accurate description, but Mathis had only heard stories about the creature.

Those stories grew with each telling. Cade had actually seen the thing in its borrowed flesh and transparent skin. Fortunately, it had only been a head, neck and torso strapped to a wooden frame. The faintest thought of such a monstrosity possessing arms and the ability to walk made his balls shrivel.

"It's called a golem," Cade said as they entered the Washington Square district. "The possibility of a trap is why we have four vans traveling in a dispersed pattern instead of two driving in tandem. And it won't be a golem luring us in. Creating such an abomination takes an extraordinary amount of magic. It would be a net loss for the Hunters if they only caught your ass and mine."

Mathis shrugged, unconvinced by Cade's math.

Braving the rain again, Cade lowered the window and stuck the tip of his tongue out, cautiously sampling the flavor of the surrounding area and its inhabitants. Palpable emotions of fear and anger coated his taste buds and soured his stomach. Beneath it all, he detected hints of feminine appeal, but none felt like his mission's target.

He jerked his head inside the van and closed the window. He didn't want to find the female in a neighborhood like Washington Square. The closer his team moved toward Onondaga Lake and US-11, the more bars and strip clubs they would encounter.

*Bars, strip clubs, prostitutes, pimps, drug dealers, junkies…*

Mathis shoved a roll of paper towels at him.

"Damn, boss, you look like you just stepped out of the shower."

"Thanks." Grunting, he dried his face then grabbed the radio set. "Tanner, anything on your end?"

Waiting for the man's reply, Cade shifted restlessly in his seat. Including his own warm body, the team comprised eight wolves and two latents spread between four vans. Everyone on the team wore charms to keep Hunters from detecting them. Another set of charms could change a vehicle's color merely by pulling a secondary charm from its silver container and joining it to the vehicle's primary charm—no witch required.

Too bad the magical assist couldn't erase the two-hundred miles of highways and city streets between their current position and the nearest clan stronghold in upstate New York.

Tanner's gravelly voice crackled over the radio. "Nothing, boss."

"Keep looking." Cade dropped the radio into the cup holder.

"Gotta take a piss." Mathis signaled a right turn half a heartbeat before he whipped the van into the parking lot of a donut and coffee shop. "You think the witches are wrong on this one?"

"You want to ask any of them?" Cade joked, opening his window fully now that the rain had paused. "We just need to wait until the target settles down for the night. Once she does, the Wonder Twins can cast for a more concrete location. After that, our noses will lead us the rest of the way."

The "Wonder Twins" were the two latents riding with Tanner. Spike and Petra weren't twins, but were siblings born a year apart. Spike was the only male latent the clan had found so far. His discovery had made everyone but Esme Gladwin, the new head of the Witches' Council, uncomfortable. She looked at Spike as proof that the Hunters intent on wiping out all shifters and witches were also latents, their ranks limited to men by choice.

Everyone else had reached the same conclusion—they just didn't turn giddy over confirmation of the theory.

"Seeing as this one came straight from Esme, I'll let you ask her, boss," Mathis answered, a smile lashed to his face. "If anyone can turn a wolf into a frog, it's gonna be her."

"She wasn't the only one casting," Cade said, stepping from the van to stretch his legs. "And she admitted something was way off about the energy. The vibe was similar to finding Petra and Spike, just significantly stronger. So it could be several latents or cubs who have banded together, always sticking close to one another."

The grin on his driver's face disappeared at the mention of potential cubs. Search teams had discovered too many orphaned wolves in the last few months, all of

6

them male and all born during a time when the fertility rate among the clans had plummeted to zero. More unnerving, the cubs appeared out of nowhere with memories as clean as the day they were born.

No question about it—Mathis and the rest of the team would much prefer to find a nubile woman who didn't realize she had enough shifter DNA in her genetic makeup to mate with a wolf and have his children. Finding a cub on the run would add another layer of dread to the already immense cloud hanging over the clans.

The thought had been rolling around inside Cade's head like an iron-spiked bowling ball the entire drive. He shoved it aside as he closed the van door and nodded at Mathis. "Hey, get me a triple shot with extra cream while you're in there."

"Sure thing, pussycat." Mathis disappeared into the coffee shop wearing a fresh smile.

Cade used the time alone to pace, loosening muscles that had cramped on the long drive and hours spent searching the city with little guidance beyond a twenty-block sector in the worst neighborhood Syracuse offered. He paced for several minutes, circling the van half a dozen times before Mathis finally exited the bathroom and ordered two coffees.

His cellphone vibrated in his pocket as he completed another slow circuit of the vehicle, jolting him from the concentrated haze into which he had settled. He fished the phone from his jeans and opened it to find new GPS coordinates from the Witches' Council. The twenty-block area had narrowed to one precise location.

Stomach dropping like a load of bricks to fill his bowels, he sent the coordinates to the wolves riding shotgun in the other vans, telling them to hold at two blocks away according to the cardinal positions he had assigned each.

In the last three months, his team had executed eight rescue missions, all of them successful. Every extraction carried its own unique risks. Not yet able to shift, a cub might be in the care of humans. A latent could be unwilling to leave with them, or she might have drawn Hunters to her. Hell, locating a latent in Washington Square meant she could be under the control of a pimp or street gang.

As unpleasant a scenario as encountering a street gang might be, Hunters were far more dangerous. Working with the precision of military strike teams, Hunters were led by a maniac named Quentin. He was their "Father General," a Dark Pope in black robes willing to sacrifice every last soldier in his war against the shifters, and his quest for power that fueled it.

Hell, there was good reason to believe he'd been kidnapping cubs for decades and siphoning off their magic. He had been caught callously referring to cubs as his "power grid." The head of the Witches' Council had been kidnapped and strapped to something like that before she was rescued.

Feeling the hairs rise along the nape of his neck, Cade

climbed into the van and plugged the coordinates into the GPS unit. The route appeared with a few lines of text next to it. A fresh growl rumbled through his chest as he read them. No cub tonight—not when the destination was a strip club. So one or multiple latents in a bar, surrounded by men and liquor with bouncers at the door and nothing but cloaking charms to shield his team from the trained killers who wanted them dead.

*Fan-fucking-tastic.*

Apprehension ghost walked the length of his spine before digging into his testicles. If he was lucky, the woman wouldn't be compatible with any of the men on his team. Otherwise, all hell would break loose if a wolf's mating response was triggered while some guy had a hand on the chick's ass.

Heaven forbid a lap dance was in progress. The scent of arousal from the human male would be as good as a signed death warrant for the dude.

Mathis opened the driver's side door, interrupting the scenarios racing through Cade's head. He handed a coffee to Cade, then climbed into the van. "Got anything?"

Bringing the cup to his lips, Cade nodded and tapped the GPS screen. "New location—looks like at least one latent. We're on lead. Everyone else is holding at two blocks out."

Mathis pulled the seat belt across his chest before noticing the scowl on his alpha's face. "Problem, boss?"

"She's at a strip club." Cade couldn't keep the snarl from his voice.

"So totally not a problem." Mathis laughed the location off, his face splitting into a glittering, wolfish grin. "You know what all the latents say—once you go wolf, you never go back!"

Seeing that the joke hadn't cracked Cade's stony facade, Mathis tried again. "Come on, boss. This might be your night to find a mate."

"Just get the van moving before the evening gets any worse." Cade checked the sidearm under his jacket, then fastened his seat belt. "I want to know what we're dealing with before any of you decide to run in with your dicks out and guns blazing."

"Or our guns out and dicks blazing."

Mathis waited for the laugh that wasn't coming.

"Seriously, dude, you should at least try to get some pussy before the decade is over," he grumbled, pulling from the parking space. "We'd all be a lot happier if you did. I mean—"

Cade responded with a side glare that cut off the conversation. Satisfied Mathis would remain silent until they reached their location, Cade eased back against the seat and kept one eye on the dashboard's built-in navigation screen while he argued with the beast inside him.

Unlike all the other latent and cub runs his team had made, his wolf had been twitching since the early morning call to action that had mobilized his team.

*The latent doesn't interest us*, he reminded it.

A tail flicked inside his skull, the fur soft as silk and

caressing him in a way that reminded Cade of his hand in the shower the night before.

*We're just here for the extraction.*

The soft tease of fur became nails scratching against his sternum. He grabbed his wolf by its neck and gave a hard shake.

*This woman is not ours.*

*Ours is gone.*

The wolf quieted at the reminder.

Cade sighed—with regret, not relief. No matter how many women the Witches' Council located, he held no illusion that he would find one with whom he was compatible.

Fact was, he'd met his mate when he was eight and she was six. But the she-wolf ended up rejecting the mating and leaving the clan when he was eighteen.

The dozen years that had passed since didn't make her any less his mate.

It was more than the shifter roulette equivalent of fated mating for him. As far as Cade was concerned, he couldn't un-promise his heart—even if the woman had never truly wanted it.

# CHAPTER 2

Lights strobed red and blue against the brick façade of the Wild Pony Gentlemen's Club. A rough-looking mix of men and women, old and young, crowded around the police tape blocking the entrance.

"Here I was worried about Hunters." Mathis strummed his fingers on the steering wheel, a disgruntled rumble coating each word. "How about we throw this one back in the latent pool, boss?"

"You know we can't."

"Actually, I don't kn—" Mathis clamped his mouth shut as Cade pushed his wolf at the man.

"This is the assignment we have today," Cade growled as he stepped from the van. "Each latent we find makes us stronger. The stronger we are, the sooner we'll solve this damn mystery with the cubs."

Cade shot Mathis another hard look, then gestured at the radio.

"Tell the others to hold position at one block and keep the engines running while I—"

The instruction died on his tongue as he caught his first whiff of the female they sought. Even unseen, she defied all expectations—neither a latent nor a cub, but a she-wolf…in heat.

A meaty chuckle vibrated low in his throat, his cock surging a hard line up to poke at his navel. "Heat" was the wrong fucking word. The woman's scent scorched his face until his tongue and balls began to sweat.

Rain or not, how the hell had anyone on his team missed her?

"I gave you an order," he snapped as Mathis opened the driver's side door. "Get on the damn radio and tell them to hold."

Mathis challenged him with a low snarl.

Cade turned, pushing his wolf until the man folded into an uneasy obedience.

*Shit.* The situation was far beyond the worst-case scenario he had imagined earlier.

The scent he was picking up told him that the woman was not only in heat, but a female alpha. Believed extinct, female alphas had always been extremely rare. For Cade, this was *not* the way he wanted to find out otherwise.

An alpha she-wolf didn't need a signature match with an unmated male to fiercely attract his attention. She only needed to be in her breeding cycle without a life mate of her own.

Meaning, instead of one lust-filled wolf threatening the mission, he would have eight.

Cade stepped away from the van. After a dozen more steps, he heard the stealthy rustle of Mathis trying to follow. He issued another growl, the sound far below the range of human hearing and meant to snap like jaws around Mathis's wolf until it turned belly up and whined in submission.

"We can't rescue her like this," he warned in a fierce whisper. "Now get in the damn van and start the engine before I take your head off! And warn the other teams what we're dealing with."

Mathis hesitated, then his gaze flicked nervously toward something beyond Cade's shoulder.

Cade turned to find a cop approaching, the man's hand resting on the butt of his service weapon.

"My fiancée's in there," Cade called out, quickly setting up the only feasible story that would explain his presence, and still keep him off the cop's radar. "I've been calling, but she hasn't picked up. Please tell me the girls are okay."

"Yeah. Can't say the same for the bouncer with a knife sticking from his gut." Maneuvering to see over Cade's shoulder, the cop eyeballed Mathis climbing into the van. "Who's your fiancée?"

"Mandy." Saying the first random name that came to

mind, Cade grinned like a former frat guy talking to one of his house mates. "She's blonde, with a really sweet set of—" His hands came up then as if balancing two heavy watermelons.

The cop snorted, buying the charade. "That would describe half the chicks in there. Phones have all been confiscated while we check for video. It'll be at least an hour before the homicide detectives release anybody or give back any devices. You need to park your vehicle if you're gonna wait."

Cade nodded, his mind running in one direction while his senses ran in another.

Hell, the she-wolf's scent was *on* the cop, along with a dozen human women and as many males. His wolf dug past the distracting odors to find what he was looking for, the woman they'd driven two-hundred miles to find.

It punched him hard, right in the gut, and swelled his testicles to the point of near pain.

Oranges and clovers.

He knew the scent like the palm of his hand.

The alpha she-wolf in heat was *his mate.*

"Iris…" Her name was a feral rumble passing his lips before he could stop it.

Already on his way back to the club, the cop executed a hard pivot, his attention hooked by the name Cade had uttered. The man's gaze narrowed at the same time his hand returned to his sidearm.

"You know Detective Wilkes?"

*Detective?*

*Wilkes?*

Cade blinked for a few seconds, each flick another layer of the complicated situation processed. He had ruffled the man's suspicion by saying the name of another cop. Only, Cade's Iris had been a sixteen-year-old she-wolf when she disappeared from his life a dozen years ago without explanation or even a goodbye.

She had been Iris North back then. If she had secured a fake ID, why not change both names?

Fuck. Had she married?

The last question struck Cade like a chainsaw to the chest, nearly knocking him on his ass. Blinking with a stunned slowness, he forced his canines to retreat once more.

"Yeah, I know Iris," he answered finally, his voice still sounding like coarse gravel, but at least more human than wolf. "Maybe if I talk to her for a second, I can get Mandy pushed to the front of the line. It might help to lighten up the other girls, too. Make them more cooperative once they know Iris isn't the sort to jerk them around."

The cop rested his hand on the butt of his gun as the woman in question exited the building, drawing his gaze like a magnet. Beyond the intoxicating fragrance of her wolf being in heat, he recognized the dark russet waves of thick hair and the creamy rounded flesh he had once caressed and nibbled at while he tried his damnedest to coax her willing surrender to his wolf.

Cade's wolf howled, very nearly forcing him to shift

right then and there. And when her nose discreetly pushed up to scent the crowd, his wolf nearly broke through again. Though he was able to keep him leashed—barely— for once, his wolf's thoughts were nearly identical to his.

*Iris North...his mate...in heat...surrounded by her fellow cops and the unmated wolves of his team...out in the open, exposed to the threat of Hunters...*

Chest tightening further, Cade nodded beyond the cop's shoulder doing everything in his power to keep his voice modulated, almost casual. "Hey, there's Iris right there. How long has her last name been Wilkes?"

Iris froze then, her entire frame as still as a statue as her nose lifted a little higher, her expression widening at the scent she'd just caught.

*His scent.*

Cade's cock thickened with the realization that she had finally picked out his unique scent from the hundred plus humans around and inside the club. Joints rolled and popped along his body, the urge to transform running just below his skin at the thought of his mate recognizing him.

"I asked how long has she been Wilkes?" he barked at the patrol officer.

Startled over the aggression in Cade's tone now, the man reached for his gun just as Iris's searching gaze finally collided with Cade's. And held.

Coarse hair popped along the back of Cade's neck and along his knuckles as he fought to restrain his wolf. Feeling his nails sharpening to lethal points, he grit his jaw and all but tackled his wolf as he shoved his partially-shifted fists behind his back.

"Show me your hands!" the cop screamed.

Cade ignored the order, every fiber of his being wholly focused on Iris.

Adding kerosene to the growing fire, Mathis started the van.

"Turn the vehicle off!" Hysteria coated the patrol cop's voice. Raising his gun, he pointed it at Cade's chest. "And you show me your hands, asshole!"

Cade grinned, one hand striking forward at super-human speed to knock the gun from the cop's grip. The man shrieked, drawing the attention of every other patrol cop around him.

More weapons were drawn. Each one pointed at Cade's chest.

Iris rushed forward at a dead sprint, each step closer magnifying her primal draw on him. Her wolf called to his, the link now a live wire of electricity making the entire fucking world around them fade away.

Her heat was his to claim. Not another wolf's and certainly not the human male protectively trailing close behind her, his soft body draped in the kind of inexpensive business suit standard for police detectives.

Pure adrenaline poured into his veins at the sight of his mate running toward him. Soon, her heat was curling around his cock just as surely as if she were stroking him from base to tip, their connection so savagely charged he thought he would explode.

Then, the maddening woman went and inserted herself between him and her fellow officers, ensuring a bullet meant for him would hit her first.

*Fucking hell.* Over a decade later and she was still testing his sanity.

# CHAPTER 3

Despite the increased chaos all around, and the blood rushing in his ears over the mere possibility of his mate getting shot, Cade heard her trying to communicate with him.

Her high-frequency supplication was broken and clearly out of practice, but he heard her all the same.

*Calm down, Cade, and I'll get you out of here.*

Cade growled over the crackled command.

Alpha female or not, the she-wolf was out of her mind if she thought she could disappear without a word for a dozen years, then throw orders at him.

His canines extended. The urge to bare them at the patrol cop and the male detective following Iris felt like hooks gouging and raising his top lip.

The only submission he would accept was hers—her heat, her body positioned chest down and ass up, her pussy dripping with enough arousal to ease his thick passage into her.

Iris stepped around the cop, again using her body as a barricade, only this time, to block Cade from harming the man as she repeated her command.

*Damn it, Cade. Stand down!*

Before he could respond, the crack of a high-powered rifle sounded.

The plain-clothes detective nearest to them who'd been shadowing Iris dropped to the ground, half his head exploding from the bullet that truthfully looked like it'd been intended for Iris. It'd caught him in the temple instead mid-stride, killing him instantly.

Iris screamed and threw her body over her fallen brother-in-arms, her hands coating in blood as she tried to drag his corpse behind the nearest car as cover. Her grief was as thick as her anger; he felt both ebbing from her in waves. Clearly, she'd been close to the dead man.

Cade shot one arm out, his hard grip seizing Iris around the waist as she reached for her gun to return gunfire—her enraged eyes more vengeful human than wolf...but all alpha nonetheless. While he empathized, he couldn't let her go after the shooter. Though he still couldn't be a hundred percent certain, from his vantage point, it'd looked pretty damning that the bullet had been aimed at her.

Which meant one thing...

*Hunters on the roof, boss!*

The words in Mathis's high-frequency came through

just as Cade saw one of his vans screeching down the street toward him.

Spinning, he yanked Iris into his side and threw his body backward as the van slammed to a stop next to him, its sliding door open and waiting. Twisting as he landed inside the vehicle, Cade took the brunt of the fall and then rolled, pinning Iris to the floor while Mathis hit the accelerator again to get them the hell out of there.

Disarming Iris while she was still getting her bearings, he tossed her gun from the van before shutting the door as another rifle shot ricocheted off the bumper. Hearing the shot, Cade threw himself across his mate's body once more.

She fought, twisting and jerking. Her fingernails swiped at him to draw thin streams of blood across his cheek as her knee angled and took aim for a direct hit at his groin.

Glaring down at her as he very narrowly missed getting his balls rammed up into his gut, he pressed a hand gently but firmly to her throat, the same way his wolf would in battle until his challenger finally submitted. Staring into her eyes the entire time, he slowly denied her air, leaving her enough to breathe, but not enough to keep fighting. "You do realize those were Hunters shooting at you, don't you?"

Swift shock filtered into her expression.

When she finally calmed down, he drew in a deep breath and then slammed his eyes shut, gritting his teeth to keep from groaning. "Baby, you're not supposed to smell like this," he rumble-purred, his thoughts clouded by her scent, the fact that they'd just been shot at a distant memory.

Iris blinked once and then shook her head, as if trying to shake off the foggy effect he was having on her as well. Surprise pulled at the sides of her face, and then a microsecond later, her plump lips hardened into a scowl.

"Get off me!" She pushed at Cade's thick chest. When he didn't budge, she pushed harder. "Now, asshole!"

"Not happening." With a warm rumble, he buried his face against her neck and inhaled, feeling not just drunk with lust, but drunk, period. Everything about his mate was so effortlessly sexy. And damn potent.

He fucking loved it.

The van shuddered as the driver took a hard right, jostling them both and finally jolting Cade out of his trance. He looked out the window and saw Hunters held positions on two rooftops, leaving the cops to scramble for cover.

Sure enough, Tanner's voice squawked over the radio that more shots were being fired outside the club.

"Two through four are clear!" Tanner squawked again, letting Mathis know that the other three vans were out of the hot zone. "Color change at the next blind alley, then going down the rabbit hole!"

Cade lifted his head and barked at Mathis. "Head for Route 5. We'll catch up with them near Verona."

With the Hunters and the cops keeping each other busy, Cade settled his weight against Iris's body, partly because he was still really fucking horny, but mostly because he couldn't let go. Not yet. Not after seeing her come so close to getting shot.

Iris resumed her struggle, managing to free her upper torso enough to be able to look out the window. "You need to take me back, Cade. That was my partner they just killed!"

*Partner.*

He growled at her use of a word too close to "mate" for his liking.

"Going back won't make him any less dead." Cade leaned in, sniffing again with the need to know just how deep her partner's scent went on her clothing.

As he dipped below the neckline of her shirt, something metal touched his lips. He jerked back, fingers glossing against his mouth to make sure it only felt like the necklace had burned him.

"You're shielding yourself with *silver*?" he snarled. Shoving his hand into her blouse, Cade yanked out a delicate chain from her neck and snapped it off at the clasp.

Suddenly, the van jerked right, the frame almost buckling as a low whine of carnal need sounded from the driver's seat, before Mathis gasped out, "*Boss,* whatever you just did...undo it *right-fucking-now*."

The "it" that he couldn't in fact undo was Iris fully unmasked for the first time.

*Holy fuck.*

With the chain broken, her heat permeated every inch of the van. Energy poured from her body, the waves turning to a carnal howl only a wolf could hear. Unmated, she was a ticking bomb ready to go off on his mission, jeopardizing her life and everyone around her.

*Unmated.*

The word pulsed like a living breathing thing in his head for a second before he crushed the errant thought of her mated status like a tin can. She wasn't unmated, just unfucked. Her leaving twelve years ago didn't change the fact that he was still her mate.

And that she was still *his.*

Snarling, Cade reached between them and tugged once at the front of her pants.

"Cade, you can't..." Iris shook her head, her deep purple gaze panicked.

If he needed Mathis to calm down in the driver's seat to finish the mission and keep Iris safe, then Cade needed to claim her.

Right fucking now.

"*Stop,*" she whispered a little more forcefully.

Fear clouded her wide gaze, so that there was no she-wolf beneath him, just a frightened woman.

Despite every inch of his skin burning with desire for Iris, Cade immediately eased his weight from her.

"Control your heat," he growled, his need for her now secondary to his need to make her feel safe. "Or I will."

Nodding, she rolled to the side of the van and sat up. Her hands closed around the silver necklace. Finding the broken clasp, she placed the chain around her neck then pinched the ends together.

Then, with her eyes burning into his, she started whispering quietly to herself.

Blue light erupted along her fingertips.

Disbelief warred with shock as he watched her work. All the while, he ground his molars together to keep silent, not wanting Mathis to get wind of what was happening.

Too late.

"Boss, why is she speaking in witch tongue?"

# CHAPTER 4

*itch tongue…*

W     Her flesh burning from the silver and the blue light that erupted with her chanting, Iris tried to shove aside the vague, unpleasant memories of the witches she had met as a child.

Except for one of the women, it wasn't the witches themselves who had been unpleasant. The troubling memories came from what Iris learned about herself in their presence.

Casting words were slippery to every shifter's ears. Wolves couldn't catch them, couldn't hold them in their minds long enough to roll them off their tongues. Wolves might be magic, but they couldn't learn or cast magic.

For Iris, her ability as a child to not only remember the words the witches used but repeat them with effect had been the first clear sign to her that she was not a shifter.

She had told no one, not even the beloved grandmother raising Iris after her parents' deaths.

The secret had saved her life the day she was forced to flee clan lands, letting her fight back with a power no one knew she had. That power had shielded her until today, when Cade Mercer stormed back into her life, his words and behavior claiming the impossible.

*He thought she was in heat.*

Absolutely, totally out of the question—she couldn't be.

The blue light dancing around her fingertips and the foreign syllables rolling off her tongue proved as much. She wasn't a wolf, wasn't one of the clan's women, even though she'd been born to a mated pair.

Even though she could smell like a wolf…

And see like one at night.

Iris looked at Cade to find him staring at her, gaze wide and his jaw tight with suspicion. She pushed the distraction away and continued the chant. Beneath her fingertips, the silver melded to one unbroken circle around her neck. She knew the moment the chain was fully restored when a fresh growl rumbled through Cade's chest and the van steered straighter beneath the driver's suddenly steadied hands.

She released the necklace, then dropped her gaze to her pants with the ripped fabric around the button. No fixing that—fabric and plastic don't respond to casting, even most metals wouldn't, just iron and silver. Sure, she could and had made a pair of shoes scuttle across the floor from where they were hiding under her bed, and she had shut a door or two, but the magic wouldn't hold.

Untucking her shirt to cover the front of her pants, she scowled at Cade. "Better?"

The answer was "no," even though he didn't utter a single word. She heard it in the hot exhalation of breath as his nostrils flared, saw it in the angry shudder that rolled over his body as his gaze narrowed.

With a nervous lick to her top lip, she patted around the right side of her waistband. Her hand closed over her badge. Unclipping it, she rolled the shield at the tip of her fingers, her gaze riveted to the curved gold edges of metal instead of the angry shifter in front of her.

Cade had every right to be angry and no right at all. He had no idea what she had done for him, just like she had no idea what lies his father had filled his head with after she escaped the clan a dozen years ago.

The air in her lungs froze at the thought of the elder Mercer. Her brain became fuzzy, as it always did when she tried to remember the details of that day. Vague images and sounds danced at the corners of her eyes and ears.

Hank and his accomplices hurting her, threatening to kill Cade and her grandmother, a piercing pain and then the magic she had kept hidden exploding, her body suddenly free from his grip, legs pumping, running hard, her flesh an alien thing that just barely followed her commands.

She sharpened her focus on the shield, her grip on it so

tight the edges threatened to slice her skin. She didn't care about the pain, knew the magic running through her body would heal her the same as if she were a shifter. It was more important to stop the panic attack that threatened while she still had a chance to convince Cade to turn the van around or at least stop the vehicle and let her out.

She looked up, her cop façade in place. "You really think you can kidnap a homicide detective with another one dead on the ground?"

He shrugged and for a second she saw the eighteen-year-old boy she had been crazy in love with instead of the hardened shifter who had thrown her into the van and clawed at her pants.

She blinked, dismissing both memories as she jabbed her finger at the back door. "That's my partner—"

Cade's growl rumbled through her body, gripping her and holding her paralyzed as he closed the small distance between them.

"I tolerated that word the first time you used it." His breath played hot over her throat as he spoke. "Don't say it again."

"Joshua—" A second growl, more menacing than the first, froze her tongue for a few more seconds. She closed her eyes, tried to control the trembling she knew he could see, if not feel. She swallowed, shook her head. "Detective Harper was—"

"He's not anything but a stain on the sidewalk now," Cade reminded her. "That bullet was meant for you. You're not going back."

"I can take care of myself." She wanted to argue further, but his head had started to move in a familiar pattern, his nose and mouth lifting to the top of her head as she heard him inhale. His face made a slow descent to pass against her ear, and then her throat.

Iris threw her hands up to block him. "Don't!"

He was scenting her for another male, one whose odors went deeper than the surface to hide in intimate places. Any such trace of a man was long gone.

"Stop and let me out," she ordered, squirming to gain a little space between their bodies.

"If I do, you'll have to give up the clan. The only way to stop the cops' questions is to give them us." His hand closed over the badge she still played with. Taking it from her, he tucked it in his jeans pocket. "You want to turn everyone over? Me? Your grandmother?"

"My grandmother's dead," she bit out, turning her head, but not before she saw shock flicker in his dark eyes.

"And how the hell do you know that?" he barked. "You visited our lands after you left?"

Wiggling away from him, she shook her head, then pressed her face against her knees and wrapped her arms around her shins.

"I saw it," she answered, her words muffled. "Felt it when she passed."

"Don't believe you," he growled, his hands continuing to move over her with all the efficiency of a street cop until he found her cellphone. "Andra swore she kissed you goodbye the night she passed. No one believed her, but her words always stuck with me. She was convinced you visited."

Iris had felt the kiss, her heart breaking at the distant press of her beloved grandmother's lips. But she hadn't been there—not physically.

Cade slapped a padlock on the side door, then moved into the front passenger seat. Rolling down the window, he tossed the phone and badge. Hearing the right rear tire smash the phone's case, Iris hugged her legs a little tighter.

"You can't take me back to West Virginia," she said, trying to project authority, but her voice shaking too violently to sound like anything other than a frightened woman. "If you take me back there, I'm as good as dead."

Cade twisted in his seat to stare at Iris.

She forced herself not to squirm, not to think about the times they had spent away from the watchful eye of her grandmother or the hateful stare of his father. She beat back the comforting scent of pine and wintergreen that had lured her out of the strip club with its dead bouncer. And as she waited for him to say something—anything— she realized he didn't care if she lived or died.

Whatever emotion had stirred within him when her necklace broke, it was the product of animal instinct. With the silver restored, she was nothing more than a mission the clan had sent him on.

"There's only one place I'm taking you, and it isn't

Virginia," he said, his voice hard as he turned to face the front of the vehicle. "You're going to the Witches' Council. They're the ones who sent me to find you. They're the ones who think you're so fucking important."

# CHAPTER 5

Two-hundred miles later, Cade opened the van's side door and braced against the look on Iris's face.

He expected anger, a blazing white fury. Instead, he discovered a trembling fear that darkened her purple gaze until it was almost black. Slamming the door shut without removing her, he turned on his heels and barked at Mathis.

"Bring her inside!" Reaching into his pocket for his house key, he slowed his steps and lowered his voice to a register he hoped Iris could only feel and not hear through the van's steel frame. "Respectfully or I'll rip your throat out."

Opening the door, Cade stepped into the house's dark interior. His hand hovered over the light switch. He didn't want the light on, didn't want to look in her eyes and see that she was afraid of him.

She had no reason to be.

He blinked, his chest tightening as he remembered holding her down in the van, his hand ripping the front panel of her pants as he fought his wolf to keep from slicing deeper.

She had to realize he had contained himself—strangled the need triggered by the ball burning, cock gripping, full-on rutting odor of a she-wolf who was not only a female alpha but his mate, a woman he had loved as long as he could remember.

A woman who had once welcomed his soft caresses and hard kisses…

With the house remaining unlit, he watched Mathis guide Iris out of the van. Her lips quivered as she said something, her face turning toward the driver so that she spoke straight into his ear.

Cade heard only one word, the only one he needed to hear.

*Hank.*

"Dead," Cade barked, his voice as cold and dead as his father. "Happened about a month after you skipped out. You wanna tell me if that was a coincidence?"

He watched as her face hardened. He flipped the lights on and pushed the door open a little more before he moved deeper into the living room. As soon as Iris crossed the house's threshold, Cade stopped Mathis with an upheld hand.

"Go to the latents' dorm and round up some clothes and supplies."

Iris turned toward the door, her hands and jaw moving as if searching for a way to make Mathis stay.

Reaching past the she-wolf, Cade slammed the door. She jerked, the silver necklace around her throat bouncing upward then catching on the edge of her blouse's neckline. His fingers itched with the need to rip off the piece of jewelry. He gripped her shoulders, uncertain of his next move.

She stiffened beneath his touch.

"Time to talk." The order rumbled through him with mixed motives. He wanted to talk her right into his bedroom, to remove the clothes that held the scent of other men, to lovingly wash her body, then bury himself between her soft thighs as he nuzzled her pale neck, moving lower to part the folds of her sex and lick her into submission.

Tightening his grip, he turned and directed her toward the couch. "Sit."

She obeyed, but instantly seized one of the oversized couch pillows and clutched it against her torso. The fleeting anger that had lit her gaze a few seconds before reverted to fear. Scowling, Cade yanked the pillow from her and nodded down the hall.

"Perhaps you should shower first," he suggested dryly. "You're getting bits of Detective Harper all over my furniture."

Violet fire erupted in her eyes as her face turned stony again.

He nodded, satisfied. An angry mate he could handle.

A fearful one clawed at his gut with a burn worse than any fire, bullet, or silver could conjure. He watched Iris rise silently from the couch, his posture stern but his every sense targeted on her until she slammed the bathroom door and locked it.

Alone, he sank onto the couch and pulled the pillow to his nose.

There were no actual bits of the dead man on the pillow or furniture. The fabric, however, had soaked up Iris's scent like a sponge dipped in perfume. The mingling of cloves and oranges with the deeper musk of her heat stirred his cock to full hardness.

Sighing, he lowered the pillow from his face, pushing it down his chest and stomach until it rested firmly against his swollen cock. The sigh turned to a growl, the sound vibrating so low he knew it would penetrate the walls and even the fall of water over Iris's soft body.

Another low, rumbling quiver of noise moved through him to pass over his shaft like a lover's fingers. Eyes closed, he imagined his mate in his shower.

For as long as he'd known her, Iris had never quite looked like a shifter, her sweet body too soft, her face too round. But he'd been able to smell the wolf in her when others hadn't—not even the grandmother raising her.

He and he alone had been able to see the shift that never fully materialized as it shimmered beneath her skin, fighting to break out.

Now, all these years later, hell, there was zero doubt

that Iris was all wolf. Just as there was no arguing the fact that she was in heat.

…And just down the hall from him, with the warm water kissing her naked body, touching her where his mouth and hands should be preparing her for his cock.

Tossing the pillow aside, Cade stood and took his first step toward the bathroom.

His right foot dragged forward, his usual iron will fighting the desire to shift. Body shaking, he took a third step, right hip dipping, ankle rolling outward as the other foot started to move forward.

A tentative knock landed on his front door.

He sprang backward, landing expertly behind the couch in a tactical position before laughing at himself. Mirth blurred his vision. He rubbed roughly at his cheek, laughing some more and shaking his head.

Maybe Mathis was right and he was turning into a pussycat. He sure as shit had just jumped like one. And how the hell did someone make it to his front door without him knowing it at the first crunch of tires on his drive?

Oh, that's right. His entire focus had been on Iris, on the lingering scent filled with her heat and the memories of her yielding flesh the last time the two of them had been alone in their youth. They had been so close to completion that time, their hands venturing beneath one another's clothing to stroke and tease where they had never ventured before.

She had climaxed, his fingers drenched with her

juices, sticky when he brought them to his tongue to taste her for the first—

The intrusive knock landed again. Damn it, of all the shitty timing. "Coming!" he barked, prowling toward the door while his wolf sought out the energy of the person knocking.

Right off the bat, he knew it wasn't Mathis on the other side of the door, whom he'd expected to return with the clothes.

In fact, the energy wasn't male at all. No, this energy was undeniably female, shifter. Not to mention unmated and trembling...

*What the hell?*

He yanked the door open to find Joelle Perry holding a small duffel bag of clothes in front of her like it was a silver shield that could protect against Cade's ire.

"Mathis said to bring this!" she blurted.

Hearing Joelle's voice shake worse than her hands, Cade closed his eyes and cursed Mathis. He understood why his second had sent someone else, but he'd made a bad choice.

Mathis could have chosen any other female wolf, or a mated male, even one of the latents. Instead, the prick had sent a nineteen-year-old wolfling who had been sniffing around Cade since her first heat—a move that reeked not of stupidity but sabotage.

Grabbing the duffel, Cade jerked it toward him. She held tight to the bag, the momentum pulling her into his house.

"Leave, Joelle. Now."

She dropped her gaze, refusing to challenge a pack alpha directly, even if Cade wasn't her alpha. He and his team were only temporarily living among the New York shifters. Joelle had been born to them.

"I thought all new latents were supposed to go to the Fielding house," she prodded, her body sidling close to his again, her small breasts thrusting forward and up to lead the way.

He could hear the question lurking beneath the little she-wolf's challenge, could see it in the way her body twitched with a poorly concealed need. She wanted to know if the woman she had brought the clothes for was a latent whose scent marked her as Cade's mate.

"My guest isn't a latent and you need to go now." He fought the urge to growl at the wolfling, knowing the energy running through his body was too confused by Iris's proximity for the sound to come out right.

The way his day was going, his mate would exit the bathroom to find Joelle on her knees, the gusset of her jeans soaked through, and her pert ass bobbing in the air in supplication for Cade to take her if he risked any dominant sound.

The girl's delicate nose lifted to scent the room. "A regular human?"

His right brow slowly rising as he breathed deeply, Cade shook his head. How could she not smell what Iris was? Did the silver mute it completely for another she-wolf? Maybe it was the water and soap covering Iris's lush body as she washed away the evidence of her dead partner?

He wanted to tap Joelle's pert nose and ask the girl if it was defective. There was no missing Iris's scent. Even with the wolfling drenched between her thighs, all Cade could focus on was his mate's smell, the cloves and oranges, the sweet, deep odor of the heat that would let him put a pup in her as soon as he could get Iris to spread her legs in invitation.

With the duffel as a barrier between them, he tried to steer Joelle out of his house. "Time for you to go, cub."

"Not a cub." A weak snarl bubbled past the young woman's pouting lips.

Just then the click of a door opening from down the hall caught Joelle's attention. Frowning, she gazed past his shoulder to see who was coming out of the bathroom.

Instantly, her gaze widened in shock, before her expression clouded over, her lip curling up. "Is that *your* robe on that…that…*woman*?"

Cade had half a second to laugh at the possessive tone to Joelle's question before a sudden blast of heat slammed into his back—the explosive wave of energy about as subtle as a wrecking ball.

*Hot damn.*

# CHAPTER 6

A sharp crackle-snap of witch light followed the blast, its energy running electric fingers through his hair and down his spine.

A second sizzling hot explosion hit the air, this time more wolf than witch.

And this time, not aimed at him.

Immediately, Joelle buckled to the ground.

Though he didn't need to glance over his shoulder to know the culprit in question was Iris, he damn sure shot his gaze her way, mainly so he could see his robe hugging her luscious curves.

His mate's russet hair, wet from the shower, clung to the sides of her beautiful face, a few strands touching lush lips as plump and sexy as the rest of her.

Dropping the bag, he grabbed the wolfling by one arm and roughly hauled her to her feet.

With his mate's wrath pushing at his back, he stumbled into the drive, dragging Joelle's half limp form with him. He shoved her into the cab of her truck, his hands ransacking her jacket pockets for the key. Finding it, he shoved it into the ignition and turned the engine over.

"Can you drive?" He barked the question as he gave the girl a hard shake to rouse her senses.

She offered a faint nod. "Who was that?"

"That, little cub, was your alpha—"

Another snarl, this time with a flash of angry canines, erupted from the wolfling.

She was right to take exception to his words, but only technically.

Joelle's current alpha and his mate were in their fifties and managing a pack of twenty-five wolves.

But he said what he said and the words felt right to Cade.

The sheer power rolling off Iris had been almost enough to knock him off his feet. And he doubted she was even accustomed to wielding it fully yet.

When Iris finally let her wolf run free? He couldn't imagine an alpha, male or female, who could stand up to her.

"That woman who just laid you out was *my mate*," Cade rumbled. "And you'll damn well treat her as such. Now get the hell out of here before she fries your ass!"

He slammed the truck door and took a step back, glaring at the girl through the window until she threw the vehicle in gear and smashed her foot down on the accelerator. Shielding his face from the loose gravel the tires kicked up, he watched until she was safely out of his drive.

Cautiously turning toward the house, he saw that Iris hadn't moved from the hallway. Squaring his shoulders, he stalked back into his house, not stopping until he was no more than a foot from his mate.

Stiff and shaking, her arms crowded her curves and ended in clenched fists. Her wolf glowed in her gaze, a glint of silver hugging the outer side of each pupil like a crescent moon.

"What the hell, Iris?" he growled. As turned on as he was at the moment, he was also royally pissed off.

An alpha she-wolf like Iris wouldn't normally react so severely if a female—a weaker one, at that—were talking shit the way Joelle had been. No, that volatile a reaction could only have been triggered by one thing.

The scent of Joelle's arousal—for Cade.

Though the wolfling wasn't currently in heat, she'd been practically dripping with unquenched arousal. Mainly *because* it was unquenched, in that neither Cade nor his wolf had ever shown even the smallest, most remote attraction for the girl.

Not that it was any of Iris's business.

*Iris* was the one who had rejected their mating. So where did she get off being territorial over him all these years later?

Iris took a step back, gaze darting in search of an escape route.

Cade growled at her retreat.

"You run away for twelve fucking years, years you should have been with me as my mate—" He raised his hand, warning against further retreat as Iris took another step away from him. "And you want to take a wolfling's head off because she drops a little juice around me?"

Lips quivering, Iris didn't reply.

Cade huffed at her, their bodies close enough that the warmth of his breath curled against her face.

The cool air sweeping in from the door he had left open did nothing to temper his anger or hot desire. He was ready to take her, didn't care if the entire world looked on, so great was his need.

He placed his palm on her shoulders, forced her against the wall. His gaze dipped to her throat and then his hand captured the silver necklace and jerked it from her once more.

*Sweet heaven...*

He let the scent of her heat wash over him, rolled with its force even as his knees turned liquid. She had always smelled so damn delicious, but this was entirely different. This was the promise of her, forever, their cubs, a stronger pack, a stronger clan. Hell, a stronger shifter nation.

His hands curled around the collar of the robe she wore. He leaned in, head angling so that his mouth could claim hers.

"No!" Her palms pushed against his chest, the strength surprising him.

The strength and the blistering sensation that came

45

with her touch. Looking down, he saw her fingernails glowing.

"More silver, baby?" Absently licking his top lip, Cade grabbed her hand. Willing one of his nails longer and sharper, he scratched at the dark purple polish Iris wore. The paint flaked away to reveal a layer of silver beneath.

He rolled his lips, more confused than ever. Wolves were skittish around silver, especially when paired with magic. Iris wasn't a witch. He could see her wolf in her gaze, smell it, almost hear it scratching around inside her skull as it whined to escape. So why was his mate wearing silver, throwing witch light and speaking in tongues?

Dropping her hand, he grabbed the collar of the robe and pushed the edges aside. "Any more silver I should know about?"

Iris gasped. The sharp intake distracted him from the top swell of her breasts, yanked his gaze upward to her trembling lips. Leaning closer, his eyes drinking in the shape of her mouth, he let his fingertips touch her bare skin. His hips pushed forward, his cock upright and hard as it nestled against the soft curve of her stomach.

Locking his gaze with hers, Cade surfed his fingers along the swell of her breasts to find one swollen nipple. Another gasp, this one shared between them as he found the thin silver rod that pierced her flesh. Thumbing it, he felt her weight shift suddenly and knew Iris remained standing only from the hard press of his body against hers.

His tongue came out, tasting the air before it rested

against his top row of teeth. Giving the nipple bar a gentle twist, he watched her eyelids flutter then shut.

He had her.

Silver or not, she would yield.

His other hand drifted down. Finding the soft fur of her sex, he parted her drenched folds, no longer surprised when he discovered more silver, this time a ring looped through her clit. The tip of his tongue quivered as he thought about snagging the ring with it, lifting and gently tugging the little piece of jewelry before he sought out the small pearl of pleasure tucked inside the hood.

His fingers and thumb did what his tongue couldn't yet do. He manipulated the ring, pushed it up once then down before his thumb rubbed a firm circle against the fleshiest part of her clit.

Mouth closing in on his mate's throat, he mumbled a question before his lips sealed around her hot flesh. "How the hell did the casters even find you?"

Some ten feet from where he stood with Iris, a feminine cough froze Cade in place.

"Well, we're marginally competent at our job—believe it or not."

Beneath his touch, Iris stiffened. The short, heavy breaths she had been gulping in as he stroked her ceased abruptly, her chest suddenly motionless. Cade moved so that his body shielded his mate. A growl rumbled past his lips, its rolling vibrations feral and protective.

Just inside his door stood Esme Gladwin, the new head of the Witches' Council. Her mate Denver stood next to her, but faced away from the scene they had interrupted. At the presence of another male shifter, fur bristled along Cade's hands and arms. His spine loosened, ready to snap and pop until he was in his wolf form.

"Don't even think about it," Denver growled, his head moving just enough to show a flash of fang and the corner glare of one topaz-colored eye.

"Oh, I'm thinking about it," Cade rumbled back.

He wouldn't lay so much as a finger on the witch. She was a friend. But Denver had barely inched into frenemy territory. The ginger-colored shifter had always been a pain in the ass, even when he'd been a pack beta in the Tennessee clan. Now that he'd been forced to step up as Esme's mate and stop downplaying the formidable power running through him, he was one snarl away from being a bloodied pain in the ass.

Esme half turned to Denver, her hand on his shoulder as she whispered sweet nothings in an attempt to calm him. When witch light seeped from her fingers to settle against his clothes, he offered a softer growl, one meant to warn without frightening.

"He doesn't get to threaten you like that—no one does."

She rose on her tiptoes, one palm curling around the back of Denver's skull so that he tilted it forward and their foreheads briefly touched.

"He wasn't," she softly corrected. "He was threatening you. Protecting her. You'd do the same."

When she had her quarrelsome mate under control, Esme looked at Cade, her expression contrite.

"I'm sorry. I sensed both an amazing power fluctuation and a high distress level..." Her hand gestured at the front door Cade had left open. "But I should have held back."

"No." Her tone cold and precise, Iris spoke over Cade's shoulder. "You were right to enter. What you saw wasn't...consensual."

Cade watched, frozen inside, as a smirk crawled up the side of Denver's face. He focused on the man's amused sneer, trying to forget the lie that had just escaped his mate's lips.

At least he hoped it was a lie.

He didn't want to think that the wet, swollen folds he had just fingered were the product of fear.

Blinking, he dropped his head, his gaze tracing the blue whorls in his carpet as his lips mashed and slid against one another. He stepped forward, no longer shielding Iris so that she had to scramble to close the robe.

Somehow, he forced his feet to keep moving until he reached the couch and plopped down.

"Uhm..." Esme gave another little cough as Iris fumbled with the robe's sash. The witch's gaze landed on the duffel, her expression brightening. "Clothes?"

Cade grunted as she swept the bag up and started toward Iris.

"I know it's getting late," Esme prattled amicably as she crossed the front room. "And it's certainly been a challenging day. But we really need to discuss what happened

—and, no offense, figure out…well, *what* you are. We were a full mile out when I felt a power spike…then some she-wolf in a truck almost hit us at the drive's turn in, and…"

Pausing, the witch barked out a nervous laugh.

"I should shut up and let you get dressed."

Cade heard the crisp brush of canvas as Esme handed the duffel bag off to a still silent Iris. He wanted to look over his shoulder at the women, to get a read on Iris's face and body language, but he knew that would only sink the blade she had just gutted him with another inch deeper.

He could feel the cold rolling off her just as distinctly as he had felt her blistering heat.

"I'll get us some tea going and something to eat while you change," Esme offered as she returned to the front room.

When the witch's gentle touch landed on his hand, Cade looked up to find Esme's face lit with a familiar and tender concern. He had a second to feel like a total shit for snarling at one of his best friends before he heard the fresh crackle of witch light from the hall and the force of Iris's wolf rising up.

Denver spun, ready to respond to any threat directed at his mate. Esme removed her hand from Cade, her other arm extending behind her, fingers splayed in a stop motion to quiet Denver. She smiled in the direction of the hall, her gaze asking forgiveness from the she-wolf at the unintended trespass. A heartbeat later, the bathroom door slammed shut.

Cade wiped a shaky hand across his forehead before releasing the breath he'd been holding at the second flare of his mate's jealousy. He didn't know whether to laugh or howl.

*Not consensual, my ass.*

# CHAPTER 7

D ressed in a stranger's bra and panties, Iris sat on the tub's edge and tried to push down the questions constantly hammering inside her head. Several wrestled for supremacy. She had heard the word "latent" several times since the kidnapping and had been referred to as one.

So…what exactly were latents and could that be what had always been wrong with her? Did they go into heat like she-wolves? Could they speak witch's tongue?

And what the hell had happened among the clans in the last twelve years that a witch and a wolf had become a bonded pair?

*Shield yourself now, get answers later…*

"Right," she mumbled, rubbing at her cheeks as she glanced one last time to make sure the bathroom door was locked. Satisfied it was, she extended a finger and placed the nail's tip against her thigh. With her other hand, she reached for the sink and turned the cold water on at full force to dampen the volume of her words.

She started chanting, the finger motionless until the nail tip started to glow.

With the blue light came heat. She scratched purposefully at her leg, lightly singeing the flesh with an image of a raven's claw.

Next came the crude shape of a hammer's head topped by horns. Still chanting, she changed thighs. The silver in the nail polish pitted magic against magic and would prevent the wards she had just drawn from healing for several days.

As the skin on her legs cooled, Iris marked her forearms with the same images just below the interior bend of each elbow.

Finished, she turned the water off and pulled on the borrowed slacks and sweater. Rooting through the duffel bag, she found a pair of dress socks and put them on before sliding into her own shoes. Then she unlocked the door, still swearing inside her head for retreating into the bathroom instead of a bedroom with an escape-worthy window.

Not that running would do any good. Cade was right about what would happen if she tried to return to her life in Syracuse. Nothing but the truth would satisfy her superiors.

Exposing any of the clans to the police was untenable. Mankind wasn't ready to find out an entire sentient species had evolved alongside it, a species that possessed superior strength, lived longer on average, could heal most wounds in a few minutes, and sprouted fangs, claws and fur when its fight-or-flight mode was engaged.

Mass panic among the humans would ensue. Anyone who had ever acted a little odd would be labeled unnatural and shot by their trigger-happy neighbor. Parents would drown infants in tubs for being born with excess body hair.

Atrocity would stack upon atrocity.

Iris had seen enough everyday lunacy as a homicide cop to entertain even the smallest hope that the human population could handle the news in a rational and calm manner.

So, she wouldn't do it—and the shifters would fight like hell to make sure she couldn't. Cade, already so full of promise the last time she had seen him, now vibrated with all the power of his inner wolf. And the other wolf, the one that had arrived with the witch and was clearly her mate, was just as powerful.

The entire clan would unite in the effort to hunt Iris down.

Well, almost the entire clan, she thought, her upper lip curling in a snarl as she remembered the sleek, silver-haired she-wolf who had dropped more than a little "juice" around Cade before he had hauled the girl out to a truck. That was one shifter who wouldn't impede Iris's escape.

Feeling her flesh ripple at the memory of the wolfling's arousal, Iris stroked her hands along her arms.

She should have added more wards, but she didn't want to draw attention to what she had done by staying in the bathroom too long. The running water wouldn't have completely blocked the sound of her words from a wolf's hearing, but neither of the men would be able to tell the witch what was said. The words were too slippery for them.

Leaving the bathroom, Iris heard Cade's voice first.

"Tell me you didn't intentionally send us into a Hunter ambush? They were already in position on at least one roof with a sniper rifle."

"I told you the energy was all off." The woman's tone sounded as if she had repeated the defense more than once while Iris was in the bathroom drowning in anxiety. "I just don't understand them wanting her dea—"

The statement evaporated as the witch spotted Iris standing in the hallway. Her brow furrowed as her gaze skimmed first across Iris's covered thighs then landed on one arm. Leaving her spot on the couch, she closed the distance, gently wrapped a hand around Iris's wrist then pushed the sleeve up before Iris could protest.

"I'm Esme, by the way. And that brooding gingery hunk is my mate, Denver. The cub in his arms is Oscar." Seeing the wards Iris had carved into her skin, the witch shook her head. "Cade told me about the chanting. You're the first wolf to cast since—"

"I'm not a wolf." Iris pulled her arm from the woman's grasp as Cade growled.

She matched the growl then retreated to the nearest

wall, her senses reaching out to determine if Cade had allowed anyone else into his home while she was in the bathroom.

That they had brought a child in was bad enough. The cub's presence was nothing but an underhanded tactic to temper her responses.

"Honey, you're a wolf," Esme sighed. "I remember rumors that you had never shifted, even though you were about sixteen when you left. I'm almost certain my mother visited you once. You might remember. Her name is Camille Stone. She has the same coloring as me but is—"

"All sticks and bones, with beady eyes and a shriveled heart," Denver finished.

A sliver of a frown crossed Esme's face, but Iris recalled Camille Stone and had to agree with the witch's mate.

"Mostly it was the clan's healer, but your mother tried once to diagnose my...malady," Iris said before snorting at the memory. "Basically, it was an entire day of crystals and chanting...like there's a cure for not shifting. As I remember, that was—"

"Two weeks before you left," Cade finished for Iris. "Did Camille say anything to you? Was that why you left?"

Esme rubbed at her eyes, witch light crackling from her fingertips. "I don't even want to think about the possibility, but Camille could have spelled her."

Taking a seat as far from Cade as possible, Iris lifted a

brow in Esme's direction. "Spelled me so I left? I'm certain that's not it. Or did you mean something else?"

Standing next to her mate, the woman reached down and stroked the black hair of the little boy. He looked up and smiled softly, his eyelids offering a sleepy dance of dark lashes before his head settled against the big wolf's chest.

Iris frowned at the exchange. She only half-minded Esme using the boy as an excuse to delay answering the question. But something else about the cub's presence made Iris itch.

She could feel her skin growing hotter from head to toe, and her fingertips buzzed with the need to release energy. But even the smallest zap of magic would be suicide around the witch's overprotective mate, more so with the cub in the room.

Pressing her palms flat against the seat cushion, Iris returned her attention to Esme, both brows raised this time to prod the witch into responding.

Esme rolled her lips a few times before her head dove in a short bob and she started to blink.

Six years working homicide had imbued Iris with an innate sense of when a woman was about to cry.

Looking at Esme, she forced her expression and her voice into something softer and far more understanding than she felt. "Please, I need to know what your mother might have done to me."

"No telling." Esme shrugged, her hand briefly erasing a stray tear. "No asking her either. She escaped almost four months ago while being transported to the Witches Council for breaking her blood oath."

Iris let the news roll over her. Breaking the blood oath usually meant death.

"We don't know what happened during the escape. The two wolves guarding her were..." Esme let the words fall away. She glanced down at the cub, ensuring his eyes were closed and his face relaxed before she drew a finger across her throat.

Iris leaned in, her professional interest awakened despite the day's events.

A powerful enough witch could easily kill one or two wolves. If the murders occurred away from other shifters, the witch might even escape to live another day—or at least four months given the stated passage of time since Camille's escape.

"We know she was spelling me for a long time," Esme continued. "Weakening my magic so I couldn't help the clan as effectively. Most recently, she kept me in a coma to prevent me from healing Denver after Hunters captured and tortured him. It is also clear that she is more powerful than she ever let on."

Iris looked over at Esme's gingery wolf mate. His topaz eyes glittered with frost over the mention of Esme's mother, sending a chill down Iris's spine. She turned her gaze away to let the pair have a moment and fixed her focus on Cade next, though it was the last place she wanted to look.

She couldn't read his expression, only felt the intense

heat rolling off him despite the distance that separated them. Part of her wanted to join him on the other couch, the warmth of his muscular body offering a façade of safety.

Truth was, being next to him was the most dangerous place for her to be. Basking in his wolf's energy, she would come undone.

He would want to know why she had left.

And why she hadn't returned on her own.

Forcing her attention back to the witch, Iris tilted her chin up to control the building panic inside herm as she said plainly, "Not healing your mate sounds like it could have just been personal. Why do you think she would have done something to me a dozen years ago?"

"There were Hunter artifacts hidden in her home. Some writings and energy crystals that I believe enabled her to communicate with them. I can feel the passage of time in her handling the stones and see it in the notes she wrote in the margins. I think she joined the Hunters before I was even born." Esme moved from standing by her mate to sitting on the couch.

Her hands captured Iris's arm, one thumb rubbing against the sleeve and flesh below in a comforting gesture. "Other than the All-Mother, I've never felt a she-wolf with energy anything like yours, even without the magic. If Camille was working with Hunters and sensed what was waiting to bloom inside you—"

"Why did you leave?" Cade blurted out finally, his

voice a deep, pained rumble. "It can't be coincidence that she visited and two weeks later you were gone."

Iris closed her eyes. Images swelled inside her head as pain and fear clawed a familiar pattern through her gut.

*Hank Mercer.*

# CHAPTER 8

The very name *Hank Mercer* still had the power to cripple her psyche. Not just because of what he'd done to her, but also because of who he was.

Cade's father.

How could she possibly tell Cade that she'd fled the clan and rejected their mating because of his own father? How could she possibly tell him what his father had tried to do or that he'd had a gang of two other wolves from outside the West Virginia clan helping him?

Simple answer was that she couldn't.

Wouldn't.

Shaking her head, she extracted her arm from Esme's light grip and stood. She didn't want to remember that day, not alone, not with the too sympathetic witch next to her, and definitely not under the accusing stare of her childhood sweetheart.

Gaining her feet, she had every urge to head for the door, but knew they wouldn't allow her to leave. Hell, she had nowhere to go if they did.

She snarled, angry at the rock and the hard place she was pinned between. Turning on one heel, she glared at Denver. "You said Hunters took out my partner?"

Ignoring Cade's soft growl at her calling Harper her partner and the way the vibration in his throat made the fine hairs on her arms stand up, she waited for Denver to nod.

"Give them to me," she continued, "and I can turn them over to my superiors. I don't need to expose the clan."

Denver offered his own snort, its tone more derisive. "If we had them to turn over, they'd be dead already. And who's to say any captured Hunter won't talk about the clan? We already know they kill any of their own in danger of being taken. The bastards have no sense of loyalty."

Lifting a hand from where he cradled the cub, Denver scratched the stubble on his cheek. "But you do have methods of finding them that we don't. Help us locate the Hunters that shot this cop of yours, and we can discuss you leav—"

Cade jumped to his feet. Just as fast, Denver stood and pushed the cub he held into Cade's arms. Denver's move shocked Iris, but, a heartbeat later, most of the fury had vanished from Cade's expression.

Cubs were too precious to the clan—that was one fact

62

that would never change. The little boy's presence had a calming effect on everyone but Iris.

Denver put his hands on Cade's shoulders and forced him down onto the couch. Smirking, he settled on the armrest next to Cade, one hand remaining on the subdued wolf's shoulder.

Eyes flashing murder, Cade glared up at him. "We should discuss this outside, you and I."

Denver grinned at him before shaking his head. "It's much more fun to stay inside and cockblock you than to shred your ass outside."

Poking his chin in Esme's direction, he chuckled. "And less distressing for the ladies and Oscar. Not to mention the logistics of coming up with a new pack leader for the group of wolves you brought with you."

Closing his eyes, Cade slowed his breathing. Watching him, Iris knew he was searching out the energy of the warm bundle of cub Denver had so purposefully placed in his arms. Somehow, the boy had remained calm throughout the exchange.

Iris glanced at Esme, her suspicions confirmed as she saw the witch's lips wordlessly moving.

Finished with her spell, Esme met Iris's gaze. Her mouth turned down, the expression sad and seeking forgiveness as she shook her head.

"Even if we found the Hunters responsible for today's death, we couldn't let you go. You don't understand the energy you're giving off. It's like pointing a laser the size of a baseball diamond at the sky. And it will get worse with each unfulfilled heat cycle you go through. More Hunters will come. They'll kill you, but only after they torture you and steal your energy to fuel their magic—"

Heart seizing in her chest, Iris stopped the witch with a raised hand. "What do you mean, fuel *their* magic?"

Gaze sharpening, Esme stood. This time, when she sought Iris's arm, there was nothing light or gentle in the way she captured it.

"Yes, *their* magic. We've known about Hunters through all the centuries they have spent trying to eradicate us." She pushed Iris's sleeve up. "But only recently have we discovered how they find us and some of the things they do when they catch a wolf...or a witch. These are Hunter wards you are carving into your skin. I recognize them from documents obtained in the last year."

A rustle of clothing and light snarls erupted from the couch. Iris risked a glance in Cade's direction to find Denver pushing a little more forcefully on his shoulder.

"Steady," Denver warned.

The warning came too late. The cub stirred and opened his eyes. He looked at Cade's face, his own expression narrowing in apprehension. Esme began to whisper, but the boy crawled off Cade's lap and approached both women.

Releasing Iris, Esme extended her arms in the boy's direction. The child bypassed her to tug at Iris's hand.

Iris tried to pull away. The cub stubbornly fisted the edge of her shirt and rested his head against her hip.

"Please," Esme whispered. "I don't want to send Oscar

back to the van with Jet and Colt. They swear too much. And their entire conversation consists of gory details extracted from their worst runs. Dead Hunters, dead and skinned wolves…"

Sighing, Iris sat and let Oscar crawl onto her lap. She finally understood why the cub had made her skin itch and burn. If she was truly in heat, the presence of a cub would trigger her den instinct.

She shook her head. The motion caught everyone's attention, but she was not about to explain herself. If she tried, Cade would argue with her.

Regardless of what he claimed, she didn't have a den instinct. Wolves did and she wasn't one, had never shifted. No fangs or claws or hair had ever sprouted from her flesh.

Whatever was going on with her body since Cade's arrival at the strip club didn't involve dens or mating or the ridiculous notion that she was a wolf in heat.

"Cubs are drawn to it," Denver said, intuitively grasping the argument raging inside Iris's head. "They know you're fiercely protective when you're in heat."

"At least when you're not fucking," Cade interrupted.

His gazed bored into her skull. Looking away, she saw his fists pressing down on his thick thighs, the knuckles white with the force he exerted to control whatever urges ran through him.

"I'm not—" Iris started.

"Just stop," Esme pleaded. She gave Iris's shoulder a

squeeze as she looked at Cade and Denver. "And I mean all three of you!"

"We don't have to deal with why you left tonight," she told Iris, pausing to glare at Cade the second his lips parted to disagree. "But it will be a long time before you can leave the clan's protection."

Esme's gaze dropped to Oscar before she lifted it to Iris and nailed the she-wolf in place with a thick curtain of tears shimmering in her eyes. "And, since you're here, you should know that there are lost cubs that need your help. Whether it's the wolf or the cop in you, I don't think you can turn away from that."

Iris looked at Cade, her grip around Oscar reflexively tightening. Victory glittered in his dark brown gaze as he saw her hug the cub closer. A smile crept up one side of his mouth, only to die a second later when Esme continued.

"I think you should stay as a guest of the Witches' Council. I can get you a semi-private room for the night, you'd just have to share the bathroom. And then, sometime tomorrow, you'd have your own keys to a one-bedroom apartment. You'd be right next to what everyone is calling Lost Cub Central." Esme raised a calming hand toward Cade at the same time Denver put a restraining one against his chest. "You know I'm right, Cade. There aren't enough resources to protect her this close to—"

"My mate only needs one resource," he growled. "Me."

Fresh heat and need washed over Iris. Cade may have

been talking to the witch and Denver, but Iris knew he had meant the growl for her alone. He had simultaneously pushed his wolf at her, warming her belly and thighs with its dominance.

Warning bells ringing in her ears, she slid the cub onto Esme's lap.

"I won't stay here," she said, looking at the floor. "But I'll go with you."

# CHAPTER 9

"You aren't convening the Witches' Council—are you?" Iris asked, her tone sharpening as she entered an auditorium-like cavern deep within the High Peaks region of the Adirondack Mountains.

"No, I just wanted someplace we could spread out with the files," Esme said, her hand flicking at the massive table that served as the chamber's focal point. "And still have some privacy—to the extent that's possible in a structure filled with shifters."

Iris turned a semicircle, looking at the seating carved into the stone before examining the wooden table and its many chairs. She didn't need to count their number. She knew from childhood stories Andra had told her that there were twenty-seven spots at the table.

One was for The Nakari, mother to all, two for the representatives of the Witches' Council, twelve for the head of each clan, and twelve for what should be the most powerful witch from each clan, but usually was the most senior witch.

Clan leaders and witches from other countries had also visited, but those occasions were rare when Iris was a teen. With human concern over terrorism growing exponentially since then, airport and border security would be more dangerous for shifters than it had ever been.

While current body scanners had a privacy filter on the display that showed a generic figure on screen at the airports, the actual images captured and stored by the government had more than enough detail to expose the existence of shifters to the world. It only seemed logical to Iris that such changes in technology had rendered global meetings obsolete.

Quieting the cop side of her brain for a second, she took a seat and stroked the table's surface. The maker had bewitched its construction—or so Andra had said.

No Wych Elm had ever grown to more than a tenth of the table's size naturally. Even more impossible were how the burlish swirls of black, gold, and reddish browns covered the entire surface.

"My grandmother described this to me," Iris said, her gaze remaining on the stormy pattern so she wouldn't have to look at the overly sympathetic witch. "It was made in the time of All-Mother Zara...."

She trailed off, realizing she should have counted the chairs—or at least glanced at all of them.

"Yes," Esme said, picking up the thread. "No one would sit until she had. She abhorred the custom and ordered wolf and witch to take their comfort if she was running late.

It was the one command they unerringly disobeyed. Disrespectful, they said. What if one accidentally sat in her favored spot? So she had a new chair built, one that was a little bigger, a little more ornate than the others. And still, they stood until she arrived."

Keeping her gaze on the table, Iris vaguely motioned at its scope.

"There are only twenty-six chairs, each the same," she said. "Why is there no seat for The Nakari?"

"All-Mother Riya died a decade ago."

Pain stabbed Iris in the chest, cut off her oxygen. She should have realized the All-Mother could no longer be alive, not with all that she had been told about the missing cubs and Hunter attacks.

"There should have been a successor—"

She shut up and focused on breathing. Esme remained silent until Iris finally lifted her gaze.

"Never located," the witch said. "Perhaps never born, perhaps her nature hidden from herself and to us for reasons unknown. Maybe that all changed today."

It took a few, elongated seconds for Esme's meaning to sink in.

Top lip lifting in a snarl, Iris shook her head. "I would expect the head of the Witches' Council to be more informed about the All-Mother. Like all other alphas, she shifts earlier than most. Worse than merely being a late bloomer, I've never shifted. And the successor's magic is there from the beginning. She is born with a witch's caul. I think my mother and grandmother would have noticed!"

The last bit came out hotter than Iris intended, hot enough to burn her fingertips with the magic she was fighting to contain as her emotions somersaulted through her.

Were the clans so desperate they would irrationally grasp at Iris like some kind of life preserver? First as if she were a female alpha wolf and, now, as if she were THE female alpha.

*All-Mother Iris…as if!*

"The presence of a caul had always been the case," Esme agreed, her tone hardening as she continued. "Until it wasn't. It could be we are facing the passing of several more generations before a new All-Mother is born. Except for the near extinction of shifters during the Dark Ages, that would be unprecedented. In all other recorded times, a female cub destined to succeed the All-Mother has always been born in time to be tutored and protected by the existing All-Mother as her heir. But, even if you are not The Nakari—and despite what forced you off clan lands and away from any other shifters—we all need you to step up."

Iris leaned back in the chair, her gaze drilling into the witch's skull.

*...despite what forced you off clan lands...*

"It was painful, I sense that," Esme soothed. "But this war is being waged against every clan in the country."

"Just this country?"

Esme shrugged. "We've lost contact since Riya's death. Calls have stopped coming in or being answered. The envoys we sent never returned and none have visited. Even within this country, each clan has been slowly transitioning toward becoming its own silo because of how dangerous travel has become."

She drew a deep breath then shook her head a little harder, a ring of witch light circling her pupils. "So, yes, we need you to put the past aside and step the hell up."

The double doors on the north end of the chamber opened before Iris could release the torrent of words that had dammed themselves behind her clenched teeth.

Her gaze landed first on Cade. Standing next to him were Denver and two of the many people she had met earlier.

The wolf with them was named Seth. He was close to Iris in age but from the Tennessee clan, so Iris had never crossed paths with him before today. The other was his mate, one of the "latents" she had heard mentioned.

Lana had been holding their son, Dash, when Esme gave Iris a tour of the facility's new school rooms. Judging by the interactions between the witch and the latent, they were best friends.

There were a few other infants around the facility, all of them younger than Lana and Seth's son. Cade had gotten close and whispered in Iris's ear on the tour that Dash was the first cub born on clan lands in more than a decade. The only other shifters born in that lost period were the orphans discovered living in the abandoned spaces of human cities.

She had seen those children on her tour, too, if only through a thick plate of one-way glass that was the same as law enforcement used in interrogation rooms. The fact that every last one was male and had dark hair startled Iris. They could have been brothers, but they were all found in different cities, some in different states, and were all too close in age.

Iris looked away from the new arrivals and the file boxes they carried, her brain trying to process everything at once—Riya's death and lack of a successor, the impossible mating of shifter to human, the orphaned cubs, the confirmed existence of Hunters, and her own changing state and how it might fit with the new, amorphous status quo for the shifters she had fled as a teenager.

"We might as well dig in while we wait for dinner to arrive," Cade said, placing his file box on the table in front of Iris before trying to slide into the chair beside her.

Esme extended an arm at the same time she pushed a generous hip between them. She reached into the box Cade had carried and pulled out a folder.

The box was hand marked *L1* in bold, black ink. Lana carried *L2*. Both boxes contained background information and interviews from all the latents discovered to date.

Snapping the folder open, Esme elbowed Cade away from Iris.

"What part of spreading out does not compute?" she asked, not bothering to lower her voice.

Turning to Iris, she smiled.

"We've tried to be methodical about the files. And comprehensive. The folders for the latents, for example, include family histories where possible." Pausing, she looked at Lana, both women's gazes instantly softening. "Lana had a younger sister. She was murdered a couple of years before Lana moved to Tennessee. The leader of the Hunters kidnapped Lana and..."

She trailed off, her mouth beginning to quiver.

"He said 'your sister Hannah didn't fight half as hard,'" Lana whispered then nodded at the two boxes. "I think about a third of the women in our files have a close missing or murdered female relative—a mother or sister. We've tried to record details on those related crimes, as well."

Stomach churning, Iris gestured at the box Seth had just placed on the table, the one that contained the files on the cubs. He pushed it closer until she could snag one edge. Pulling the lid off, she removed the thickest folder and three of the thinnest

"I'm sorry about your sister," she said.

Lana nodded but didn't meet Iris's gaze.

Taking the woman's reaction as permission to move on, she tapped the files she had pulled from the box.

"While I am a homicide detective and worked other

Crimes Against Persons before that, I thought I'd start with Oscar's file because it is the most developed and also the files for the newest cub rescues because their evidence is the freshest."

Iris pressed her hand to her mouth, several fingers rubbing hard at her lips before she stopped and shook her head. "I understand that recovery of the cubs only began after you discovered Hunter manuscripts. Something about that doesn't feel right."

"How?" Denver asked, his gaze fixed on the thick file Iris held.

She understood the reason. The cub had become Denver's—not just a foster child but as much a part of his soul as the children Esme would one day bear.

Judging by the dark glitter in his topaz eyes, he had no interest in finding Oscar's parents, especially since the cub had no memory that extended past the day Denver had discovered him.

"I can't pretend to understand how casting works." Iris folded her hands on top of the file. "But from what Lana demonstrated earlier, it sounds like a curtain being jerked back each time one of the cubs is located. No parents are found, but the boys haven't been abandoned or lost long enough to get pulled into the human world. No police, no Child Protective Services, no Good Samaritan or, the likeliest scenario of all for a child left on the streets..."

Iris paused, the pulse at her throat accelerating as she closed her eyes and spit out the distasteful words. "A sexual predator."

"If you're suggesting that all the rescues were meant to be ambushes, then they failed." Denver gestured at the box. All total, there were about two dozen files. "We've never had an unsuccessful cub mission."

"Maybe we only found them because Hunters were casting for the cubs at the same time?" Esme's mouth corkscrewed in concentration. "Like the beacon boost I seemed to have had in locating Iris today? Only, with the cubs, we lucked into getting there before any Hunters."

"That's ignoring the possibility that I was also being used as bait." Iris shook her head. "Even if I wasn't bait and some kind of beacon boost explains the curtain effect, it doesn't explain the rest. I mean—the cubs are only more vulnerable without their parents, not more discoverable."

Esme rubbed at her eyes. "So you think the cubs are bait of some kind, even though there were no Hunter attacks during their rescue?"

"I think it's a strong possibility." Reaching out, Iris placed a hand on the witch's.

Catching Cade's eager gaze on the point of contact, she pulled back. His wolf pushed at Iris, probing for something she couldn't pin down.

Did he think she was making a friend? Did he desperately want that to happen?

She'd set him straight later—if there was a later. All she had done in touching the woman was make an effort at developing rapport as an investigator.

Iris shifted her attention to Denver. While Esme led the Witches' Council, she and her mate had arrived during a power vacuum in the New York clan. Denver had filled it. That left him in charge of what happened with the cubs.

"I'd like to interview the children."

"You mean interrogate them," he snapped. A smile that looked forced surfaced and died on his lips in the space of a heartbeat. When he spoke again, he managed a polite tone. "They've been questioned multiple times."

"I thought you wanted a cop—someone with different methods?" Pushing the files away, Iris leaned back in her chair. "How many child abuse cases have any of your teams worked? How many kids have they interviewed with a mother's dead body in the next room naked… stabbed…strangled? How many—"

Denver's growl cleaved away the rest of her argument.

"She's right," Cade intervened. "If the cubs are bait, we need to know. We risk lives each time we leave the protection of our lands."

Esme nodded, as did Lana and Seth. Denver signaled his assent with a small drop in his gaze before he stood.

He nodded at his mate.

"I need to go," he said. "The other clan leaders need briefed. Whatever they decide for their people, the New York teams won't stop rescuing cubs. We'll just take more precautions."

Forgetting her resolution to ignore Cade, Iris risked a glance in his direction. He hooked her gaze before she could look away. And then he pushed his wolf at her. This time it was a gentle nudge, as if he only intended to have his energy comfort her.

The effect was the exact opposite.

"One more question," she said, stalling Denver's departure. Once one of them peeled away from the table, the others might follow until she was left alone with the stubborn wolf who insisted she was his mate. "Is there any pattern in who has been able to locate the cubs while casting?"

Esme looked to Lana.

"Just you," Lana said, her gaze remaining on the witch. "I've found about a dozen latents, as have some of the witches. Camille's casting…well…"

With the conversation threatening to come to a screeching halt at the mention of the traitorous witch, Iris quickly tried to redirect everyone's attention.

"Are all of the found cubs housed here?"

"No, just most of them," Esme answered. "There are three in California and two in Washington State. We didn't want to risk transporting them such a distance. It's impossible to tell, at the moment, if we would find more cubs if our casting location ex—"

Denver stopped his mate with a low growl. Iris glanced between the two, sensed the topic was a frequent sore point with them.

"Who knows how many cubs are being left unprotected on the streets," Esme continued, redirecting the conversation before pinning Iris with her sea green gaze. "I'd like to teach you to cast—and soon."

When Iris hesitated to respond, Cade fixed that intense

gaze of his on her and pushed the way only he could. "You gonna fight your witch as well as your wolf, baby?"

How on earth was it that Cade knew exactly what to say to rile her up even after all these years apart?

And why the hell did his challenging her every chance he got turn her on so damn much?

# CHAPTER 10

Hours later, Iris found herself bolting upright in bed, her brain and senses refusing to cooperate with one another. The scent of an unfamiliar woman clung at the room's edges despite the fresh linen that covered the mattress and pillows. Her gaze swept left, then right.

Small desk, a dresser and wardrobe. TV stand and television. Empty bookshelf.

Not her efficiency apartment in Syracuse, not a hotel.

She lifted her hand to the back of her head, fingers combing through her hair. The crack of a rifle had woken her, but the sound was a phantom, a cruel echo of the day before.

There were no blood-coated nuggets of Harper's flesh to remove, just unruly tangles with nothing more than her fingers to tame them.

Collapsing against the mattress, she forced her heart to

slow. Even with her body supine, her head pounded from too long a day followed by too little sleep. She remembered dinner at the great table in the cavern as she read through the case files and jotted down notes.

Cade had remained, so had Lana and Seth.

Hard as she had tried, Iris hadn't been able to shake Cade. He knew the witch too well, knew what approach to take with her and the others.

With everyone convinced that Iris was both in heat and capable of strong magic, very few males could be trusted by the clans to guard her. Essentially, the guard in question would have to be a very powerful shifter who was already mated...*or* the stubborn ass that was taking every available opportunity to remind the packs that he was Iris's mate.

Rolling over, she buried her face in the pillow and forcefully exhaled, the scream she wanted to release remaining ruthlessly locked in her throat.

While Cade had looked maddeningly happy with his victory after officially securing the right to be her full-time guard, Iris was anything but. She had tossed and turned relentlessly for hours after turning off the light, her thoughts alternately haunted by old nightmares and fresh images of Cade and the unfairly enigmatic wolf he had become.

In fact, it was more than simply images assailing her thoughts. With all that sexy, protective intensity coming off of him in waves from the next room—with nothing more than a shared bathroom and a locked door separating them—she found she was acutely able to sense Cade every time she woke.

From hearing him and smelling him, to then being able to *feel* him the more she became in tune with his nearness. It got to the point where she could even feel the change in the rhythm of his heartbeat during the short scheduled timeframe he allowed himself to sleep, just as she could feel when the blood flow in his veins would respond to his thoughts. His dreams.

…And every hot, vivid fantasy he'd have.

It was torture.

Yesterday's nightmare momentarily forgotten, Iris pushed a hand between her legs and pressed. The sensation too sweet and persistent, she knew no amount of pressure could extinguish the sensual burn.

*No.* Just no.

She would have to mentally push through it. She absolutely would *not* allow herself to stroke herself to try to find a tiny fraction of relief. If she did, Cade would hear or smell her efforts and assume the strokes were inspired by his presence.

Of course, he'd be right in that regard, but she definitely didn't need him knowing that.

Iris had known something was changing in her body for a while now, even if she disagreed with Cade's assessment that she was a wolf in heat for the first time.

True, she couldn't argue that her moods recently had become more volatile lately. And yes, her already-sharp senses had intensified, as well.

But she could argue that was simply her wolf growing in strength.

The most damning evidence supporting Cade's theory about her being in heat, however, was the one she'd been mulishly denying since the moment she'd scented Cade's presence outside of the strip club for the first time in over a decade.

All at once, arousal unlike anything she'd ever experienced before had crashed into her like a giant, violent tidal wave of lust.

The entire drive away from the club, her sex had clenched with an urgent need to have him inside her— right there in the van—even with his driver mere feet away. Frankly, only fear and a long ago waking nightmare had kept her from succumbing to the blinding need that had plagued her all night.

And nearly every passing hour since.

Growling, Iris turned onto her side, ears pricking at the sound of a shower running and the groan of water through pipes that were probably twice her age and twice again.

She frowned. Had the shower been running all along? If not, when had it started?

*Getting sloppy, North.* She should have heard the water when it started or realized it was running when she first woke.

In fact, her hyper-tuned senses should have told her not only that Cade was in the shared bathroom, but also the number of people roaming the dorm's halls. She should know their mood, whether they had consumed alcohol or any other intoxicant, if they were sick, terrified or angry.

But with her thoughts fixated on Cade, Iris hadn't been able to sense beyond the bedroom in which she had spent the night.

Honestly, the man's very presence was a menace to her senses. And absolutely brutal on her self-control.

*Not to mention the things that gruff dirty-talker is able to do to her libido without even touching her...*

Iris told her brain to shut up and stick with the program. No thinking about Cade's effect on her. Period.

Rubbing sleep from her eyes, she swiveled until her feet touched the floor. She glanced at the dresser opposite the bed and the mirror atop it. She looked a mess, but she really shouldn't care. If she wanted Cade to drop his fated mate mission, she needed to start going on the offensive. As in she literally needed to be offensive to the man.

The worse she looked, and the more annoying she could be, the sooner he'd move on. In theory, at least. Being stubborn had always come naturally to Cade.

Said the pot to the kettle.

At least she had a plan now. She liked plans. Feeling an actual smile starting to tug at her lips, she began a mental checklist of all the truly annoying things she could do to work his last nerve.

A nagging harpy at the bathroom door telling him to get his ass out so she could start her lengthy evening beauty product routine—which she'd have to study up on to be able to sound remotely believable at it—was a good place to start. Men hated diva behavior, right? She certainly did.

And like it or not, she and Cade were very similar. Which meant she had a pretty good idea of the most *spectacularly* irritating ways to get under his skin.

Heck, even if this plan ended up being unsuccessful, at least she'd get to drive him crazy some; it was only fair given how damn skilled the aggravating man was at testing her sanity.

*What could possibly go wrong?*

# CHAPTER 11

S miling more broadly, she untangled the covers from her waist, stood and grabbed the bathroom supplies that came with the room and the duffel bag of clothes the ridiculous she-wolf had dropped off at Cade's.

Iris slung the bag over her shoulder, unlocked her side of the door, then raised her hand to knock.

Before she could land the first sharp rap of her knuckles against the wood, however, her knees went weak. A wild, violent shudder swept through her, tingling all her nerve endings and pulsing her core.

Immediately, she bit her tongue to keep from gasping. And moaning. The bastard had been taking care of himself in the shower, stroking, squeezing...

Heart racing, she braced one hand against the wall to keep from breaking down the closed door to join him as the sensation of a hot, turbulent orgasm ripped through her.

Not her orgasm—Cade's.

By his own hand.

She slammed her eyes shut to try to stop her imagination from torturing her any further. Only to have them shocked open a second later when the bathroom door jerked inward, revealing Cade in nothing but a towel around his waist, with the water still running in the shower behind him.

Her gaze skipped away from his fierce expression to take in the broad, powerful chest covered in protective tattoos with dark, wet hair matting against his skin. Powerless to stop it, her attention then dipped to his navel, then lower still to where the hair narrowed into a line that traveled below the towel.

Her eyes ran over every droplet of water clinging to his skin, until she saw the single thick pearl of liquid on his muscled abdomen just above the long, hard erection fighting to push free and unravel his towel.

Instantly, her mouth flooded with need.

Trancelike, she swiped a finger against that bead of liquid and brought it to her lips. Her already shaky legs buckled as she took a panicked step back, shocked over her actions—and how savagely she wanted to do it *again*.

Just that quickly, her knees gave out, but Cade caught her before she could collapse to the floor.

The water coating his skin penetrated her nightgown

as he wrapped his arms around her and growled, "You don't get to run after doing that, baby."

"Doing what?" She looked up, floating in a fog of arousal that was only getting worse now that she could hear him as well as see him.

*"Tasting me,"* he rasped, his voice deeper and more feral than she'd ever heard it. "You don't get to run without letting me do the same to you, mate."

Still holding her upright, Cade walked them into her bedroom. In a haze, she felt her legs move with him, felt the hard bulge of his cock, his body heat through the towel, and her wet clothes sucking at her skin. He pushed her onto the bed, the towel falling from his hips as he bent forward.

With his entire physique being so big and powerful, it came as no surprise that his cock was equally impressive. Almost intimidatingly so.

As she looked her fill, more of his cum leaked from the small slit, the stream too steady for beads to fully form. She pressed against his chest as indecision rolled her lips. Something clawed inside her, wanting out. She shook her head, but could see that Cade was too far gone to accept any weak protest she might make.

To be fair, it wasn't like she could actually shape the word "no," especially when her entire body was fighting against the mere thought of denying him. Because the truth was, she was too far gone as well. Vicious need poured through her veins, clenched her core.

Made her moan his name quietly.

Growling at the sound, Cade pushed her gown up. His fingers curled around the gusset of her panties and then he ripped them from her. Unable to wait another second, he dipped two thick fingers into the wet evidence of her arousal and brought them to his mouth.

He tasted her then, just as she had tasted him, his eyes almost euphoric—and nearly all-wolf.

With her juices clinging to his hand, he clutched at her hips and then his cock thrust into her in one hard, deep stroke.

His wolf knot formed immediately, stretching the flesh just inside her pussy. She opened her mouth, sucking in gulps of oxygen that burned her lungs as if she had sucked in fire. In the best, most intense possible way.

Cade sealed his lips against hers, his tongue invading with the same force as his cock. His thick fingers wound through her hair, holding her in place as he kissed and fucked.

The kisses dipped down to her neck. She felt the threat of fangs against her skin. A moan, her own, blurred her vision.

"Shh, love." His kisses gentled, which slowly decimated her. Tenderly, he cupped her cheek to stare into her eyes, but she averted her face with what strength she could manage to keep her last remaining walls of resistance up all around her heart.

Her lips quivered as she fought her body's exploding response. Her breath came in short pants, the air passing her lips blue with witch light.

Cade kissed along her throat and the top of her shoulder. "Let go, Iris."

His words confused her. She was fighting like hell not to wrap her arms and legs around him, not to lift when he dipped or throw herself against him like the surf at high tide when his hips slowed to tease her sex with soft little rolls.

She wasn't holding on.

There was nothing to let go of.

He pulled back, the wolf knot ensuring he wouldn't slip out, but allowing him to sit on his haunches. He wrapped her thighs around his hips and stared down at her exposed pussy, and gorgeously pink clit. His thumb landed gently on her flesh where the silver ring pierced the thick, glistening hood.

His tongue pressed restlessly against his top lip. He met her gaze, his thumb toying with the clit ring and the tender spine of need it penetrated.

"All night long I dreamed of touching you…my mouth here..." He pushed harder against the sensitive nodule and its metal ornament. The pleasure his touch created forced her hips up. His cock tugged inside her, the knot refusing to yield its position.

Iris brought her arms up to cover her face. She didn't want Cade to see her coming even if the play of a blue hazy light over her convulsing body exposed her pleasure.

"You can't hide, baby." He rubbed harder at her clit, the resulting jerks of her body more violent as her flesh coiled around his cock. "Neither can your wolf. I see her —I've always seen her."

Still shielding her face, she shook her head. She had no wolf, the blue light proved as much. Whatever she was, it was neither wolf nor human. Her ability to sense like a wolf and heal like one came from her magic. That left her a freak among mankind and the wolves—even among the witches.

Cade exhaled, his whole body suddenly immobile. Iris couldn't subside. Her hips moved in a small circle, all the motion in the room hers beyond Cade's breathing. She wiggled, dipped, rode his cock and the thumb he kept firm against her clit. The knot and fat head stretched her pussy with each thrust she forced against him. She could feel their round, unyielding mass crowding and stroking as a shock wave of release exploded through her.

"Enough!" Cade barked. He pushed forward, sinking deeper. His hands wrapped around her wrists, jerked her arms above her head. He stared into her eyes, his wolf glowing in his gaze as he began to make shallow pumps against her mound. "You're going to look at me the next time you come and that sweet pussy goes crazy."

She tried to shut her eyes. His growl forced them wide.

"I can see her hiding inside you."

She shook her head. Other than the big cock she had locked around, Iris had no wolf inside her. If she accepted otherwise, then she had stayed away from her pack—from her mate—for a dozen years with no reason. She hadn't been beside her grandmother as the woman died. All those years would have been wasted.

"Baby, she wants to howl." Cade kissed her.

This time she didn't seek to evade his lips. She groaned down his throat, fresh tension stacking between her thighs. He sank deep, the pressure of his thick shaft making her eyes roll up. His back contorted in a way only shifters could move.

Feeling the wolf knot swell bigger, Iris cried out. She knew what came next, needed him out of her, but her body conspired with Cade. She arched against him, her moans urging him on, her whimpers a plea for him to release inside her, to fill her with his fluid and all its potentialities.

Cade bit lightly at Iris's lips, his tongue curling along their interior side between nips. He grew still. His broad chest rose and fell in deep breaths.

She opened her eyes, stared into his. Just as when he had frozen earlier, Iris couldn't stop moving against Cade's body. Her pussy hugged his shaft, sucked and squeezed at the head and knot, coiled around his entire thick length to twist greedily at his cock as it grew another impossible inch.

Her flesh at the brink of another release, she watched as more of Cade's wolf crowded his gaze, his eyes gleaming like molten silver the closer he got to losing control completely.

She exhaled a shivery breath of pure witch light at the thought of him so wildly untamed, and he growled, sealing his lips over hers, drawing in every last glowing spark until their groans of pleasure turned downright feral the instant they both hurtled over the edge.

She felt the hard jerks of his cock, felt the knot pulse with each jerk, momentarily losing volume before inflating fuller, stretching her a little more, making her already snug folds caress him even tighter.

Cade buried his face against her throat, his muffled words incomprehensible but the tone loving and sated. Her senses were hit with a sudden attack of what felt like all the most powerful allergens in the world combined— the closest she could ever come to tears—as she waited for him to unknot.

She wanted to believe that something had changed, but she was no more a wolf than when she had first erupted from sleep that morning. And no matter what Cade believed, no matter how many shifters took latents as mates, she would bear no cubs and no clan would accept her as one of their own.

The wolves in West Virginia had been given sixteen years to accept Iris. They never had. She had been shunned or ignored by all but her grandmother and Cade, their lives made more dangerous because they cared about her, wanted to keep her safe.

Still knotted inside Iris, Cade lifted his head from her shoulder. His hands gently brushed away the sweaty strands of hair that plastered her face. Seeing the tears she had shed, he thumbed their glistening line and pushed deeper, his cock and mouth seeking to keep the next tear from forming.

"It's okay, baby," he told her in a raw whisper. "Your wolf will come out next time."

Just like that, all the warmth lingering in Iris's body fled at his words.

# Chapter 12

That last whispered sentence, however kind his intent, just confirmed for Iris that nothing had changed.

Cade would always be looking for her wolf, expecting it each time and disappointed each time, even if he didn't show it and never spoke a word of admonition.

He didn't want a latent or a witch. He wanted a wolf.

He wanted what she simply couldn't be for him.

She shook her head, her gaze warily avoiding his face. "No, it won't."

"Maybe not with all this silver on." He moved to kiss her, but Iris evaded his mouth.

Seeming to realize then that something wasn't right, Cade looked at her, his dark gaze bouncing around the landmarks of her face as if trying to read her thoughts, pinpoint why she was pulling away emotionally, even though she couldn't yet physically.

Turning her head, Iris stared at the empty bookshelf waiting to be filled by the room's next occupant.

"It won't happen," she repeated, re-arming herself the only way she could. "I'm not like you, Cade. I'm not an animal."

Iris expected the words to push Cade away immediately, expected him to storm out. She sensed he wanted to. But, first, he had to unknot.

She tried to relax, tried to make his exit from her body easier. She closed her eyes, locked her jaw. Her thoughts skipped around.

She had left the clan when she was sixteen with nothing more than the shredded clothes on her back and a deep wound in her chest. But she wasn't naive about shifter sex.

Other young women in the clan liked to talk about it when she was around and the males weren't. "Balling the ball," they had called it, or the "anchor and the ladder."

They discussed often enough how best to keep teasing their mates, so the male would have to spend more time inside them.

Truthfully, Iris couldn't imagine anything more awkward once the tender affections were exhausted.

And there were certainly no tender affections in her borrowed bed.

Both her body and Cade's remained stiff as they waited in silence. Eyes still closed, she couldn't see him staring down at her, but she could feel his hard gaze.

Hoping to drive away the sensation, she replayed past lovers, paltry as the number was.

There was a one-night stand with a stranger she had made the mistake of bringing home. Then after that, the single time with her partner, Harper, the two of them desperately clinging together at the end of the first night of a terrible homicide investigation that had, for both of them, if only for the moment, erased their faith in humanity.

Both encounters had been awkward and tense, but at least she hadn't experienced "can't get my penis out of you" weird.

Until now.

Eventually, Cade could slide his still-hard, still-huge shaft out. And he did so in silence, pulling out, then sitting for a second on the bed, feet on the floor, elbows on his knees as his hands cupped the back of his head.

With a slitted gaze, she watched as a few more seconds passed before he reached for the towel, scooped it up, then stood.

He didn't bother to cover his nakedness or look at her. She studied the contours of his bare back, the broad, muscular shoulders, the torso tapering down to his waist, then the body expanding again at his powerful ass and thighs.

Half out of view in the bathroom, he reached into the shower and turned the water off then disappeared completely, the door to his room softly shutting.

Iris waited for the sound of the lock to click into place.

It didn't, but he left his room a few minutes later, his footsteps falling flat and heavy as they echoed down the hall.

Not wanting to feel Cade's release slicken her thighs when she stood, Iris waited with her eyes shut and her muscles slowly relaxing.

Sleep should not have visited her, but it did.

But with sleep came the old nightmare, its familiar hooks digging into her flesh and dragging her toward despair.

# CHAPTER 13

irt clogged Iris's mouth and nose. Her throat convulsed. Her gut twisted with a choking need to vomit as fat clumps of soil and grass cut off her supply of air.

Unidentified things wriggled and crawled against her tongue and gums, nestled themselves between her cheeks. A heavy knee pressed on her spine, pinning her body in place.

A hand threaded through her hair, jerked her head up.

Spitting out dirt and insects, Iris found herself staring straight into a long, deep hole.

Two unfamiliar males positioned fifty-gallon drums next to the freshly dug grave. Thick rubber gloves covered their hands. The liquid sloshing inside the barrels hissed each time it breached the bung cap and kissed air.

The liquid had an acrid smell to it, but the stench was

nothing compared to the odor coming off the two males handling the barrels.

Their foul, reeking flesh was the least of Iris's worries. Hank Mercer was going to kill her, put her in the ground, then destroy the evidence and her scent with some kind of acid.

Before that, he would degrade her. With his pants already unzipped, Hank's plan on how to humiliate Iris was obvious.

His claws ripped at her pants, shredding the fabric and the first layer of skin beneath.

"Kill her already," one of the helpers shouted. Sweat poured down the man's face despite the cool weather and stiff breeze.

Damn, she wished the air would blow in a different direction. She needed to think and she couldn't with the stink weighing so heavily around her.

It was worse than the dirt she had swallowed or the insects. Her stomach convulsed with the need to vomit, the physical imperative to empty her stomach eroding any chance of formulating an escape plan.

"Why?" Hank laughed. "Not like this bitch is gonna shift on me."

That was it—the reason Iris would soon be dead. She couldn't shift and Cade Mercer wanted to spend the rest of his life with her anyway. Hank had other plans for his son.

Big plans.

Hank expected his only child to replace him as pack

leader, to maybe even become clan leader one day. And that would never happen with Iris by Cade's side.

Flipping Iris onto her back, Hank shredded the blouse, gouged channels in her pale, soft flesh. At last, she experienced a sensation capable of blocking out the foul odor of the other men.

Iris screamed.

Pain rolled her eyes back in her head, but not before she saw one of the two outsiders staring at the blood, his mouth slightly ajar and a quiet, mesmerized smile plastering his face.

Something about the twisted smile adrenalized Iris. She swung a fist at Hank's head, every ounce of her flagging strength focused on landing one last shot.

Her hand connected with Hank's cheek. The blow only doubled his rage. He punched Iris in the face, his fist landing like a sledgehammer.

The cartilage in her nose snapped slow and wet, like green twigs stepped on after a morning rain. Blood spurted a crimson plume. Droplets landed in her eyes, her entire vision painted red.

One of the outsiders, the sick bastard who had been watching with fascination, kneeled next to Hank. He had a knife of some kind, long and with a blade more narrow than she had ever seen. Bending toward Iris, he reeked of a thousand corpses.

She was about to be a thousand and one.

"Silver?" Hank snarled when he saw the man's dagger.

"You dumb ass motherfucker! Get that the fuck away from me!"

Ignoring Hank, the man stuck the edge of the blade against Iris's throat. Its blade felt dull, but her skin immediately began to heat and tingle from the contact.

The sensation quickly spread along her body, zipping and humming in her head and along her limbs. The fine, almost invisible hairs on her neck and arms rose as if she were standing in the middle of a field during an electrical storm.

The tips of her fingers went numb, then blazed white hot. The air around her cracked and sizzled. The two strangers fell to the ground, their bodies engulfed in blue flame. Light of the same hue danced in the palm of her hand as she reached for the abandoned blade.

Hank reached it first, wrapped one meaty hand around the hilt, then buried the tip deep into the left side of Iris's chest.

Searing heat engulfed her flesh. The air *whooped* as it exited the pierced lung. With another zap of energy, the light jumped in a tight ball from her palm to break Hank Mercer's nose and flatten one cheekbone.

His head snapped back. His stunned body fell to the side. Pulling the blade from her chest, Iris rolled toward Hank and slammed the entire dagger, point first, into his gut. She yanked the blade from side to side, the thumb of her other hand trying to gouge its way through Hank's eye and into his brain.

Shrieking filled her ears as the two other men burned.

The flames jumped from the body closest to her to the barrel filled with acid. The air turned poisonous, burning her eyes and throat as the acid bubbled along the rim of the barrel's cap and the entire container bulged.

Releasing Hank, Iris tried to stand, every neuron in her brain firing with the command to RUN as fast and far as she could.

Her legs wouldn't obey. They folded beneath her. She clawed at the ground, pulling and pushing, her torso thumping against the dirt like a landed fish.

A hand seized her ankle. She looked over her shoulder at the murderous gaze of Hank Mercer, respected pack leader and father of the man she loved.

"I'll kill him if you come back," he snarled. "Him and that bitch grandmother of yours..."

She kicked with her free foot. The shoe connected with Hank's broken face. His grip slipped. Grabbing the hilt of the silver blade, he pulled it from his stomach, the flesh protesting wetly as it was forced to release the metal.

He was healing faster than Iris could hope to match. Tears of pain, still tinged scarlet from the blood spilled, filled her eyes as she forced her legs to lift her mass and move forward in a stumbling race away from certain death...

## CHAPTER 14

A hard knock on her room's door jerked Iris out of her nightmare and onto her feet.

Her hand instinctively searched for the pistol Cade had stripped from her days ago. Half caught in the nightmare from which the knock had woken her, she could feel Hank Mercer's hot breath on her back as she ran, her lower limbs like spider legs, everything disjointed and disobedient.

The knock sounded again, jerking her fully awake. She glanced at the clock. Almost two hours had passed since Cade left her alone and cold in bed.

She was supposed to be showered and dressed, breakfast in her gut, and already at the residence of Esme and Denver so she could interview Oscar in a relaxed, familiar setting.

Whichever wolf was at her door had come to take her there because Cade wasn't coming back.

Not after she had called him an animal.

She snatched a robe from the pile of borrowed clothing, cinched it tight, then cracked the door open. A lanky wolf somewhere in his late forties stood in the hall, a coffee tumbler in each hand.

She recognized him. Mitch Tanner. He had joined the West Virginia clan after Iris had escaped. Esme had given her a brief rundown on his history as it related to a horrifying attack Hunters had executed on a small enclave of shifters in northeast Tennessee.

"You're here to take me to the interview," she said, trying to push the nightmare of Harrow Mill out of her head and not stare at the scars on the wolf's face and neck that had been left by magic-infused silver buckshot and a long delay in reaching a healer after the attack.

Tanner nodded, his expression growing irritated as her gaze continued to scrutinize his flesh.

"I need to shower first," she blurted, mortified by her inability to look away and the knowledge that Cade's scent lingered on her body. "Give me about five minutes."

She shut the door before he could object to the extra delay.

Anticipating a night of restless sleep, she had picked out the day's clothes the prior night and placed them in a folded pile atop the room's only chair. With the air inside the cavern system averaging a constant sixty-eight degrees Fahrenheit, she had selected a thick chenille sweater and heavy denim jeans. Not only would the outfit be comfortable and warm, but Oscar would find the sweater's soft fabric less intimidating than more formal clothing.

Not that she had formal clothing to choose from.

Her days as a well-dressed homicide detective were dead and gone.

Piling her hair into a loose bun, Iris stepped into the shower, her movements quick and efficient as she washed. Three minutes later she was in front of the sink, brushing out her hair while her body air dried.

Finished, she studied her naked form for a few seconds in the mirror, hoping to memorize it in case there were any changes after what happened between her and Cade. The last thing Iris wanted was for someone to smell a pregnancy on her before she realized herself.

*What happened was you fucked him*, a sharp voice clawed at her. *You fucked him and you liked it. We liked—*

Shaking her head, Iris fled the bathroom and slammed the door behind her. The clothes went on in a jumble, the first attempt at sticking her leg through one of the pant legs revealing she had grabbed hold of the sweater.

She swore out loud then cursed silently in her head because she didn't want every damn wolf in the clan to know her business.

Something rolled happily in her gut.

*They can smell our business on us. You could have showered all day and his scent would remain.*

"Shut up!" she hissed.

No words of retort responded, but she felt a flick low in her gut.

Something was there waiting for her to welcome it.

Opening the door, she shook her head, denying the existence of whatever "it" was.

"You saying you don't want the coffee, Miss North?" Tanner asked, one arm extended with a tumbler in it. "Promise it's still hot."

Iris forced her professional mask into place and smiled as she claimed the offering.

"Rough night?" she asked before taking a sip. "I heard one of the other teams brought a latent in for healing. Michelle?"

Tanner's mouth twitched.

"Of course you heard." He inclined his head one door down. "You were in a room *next* to your mate when I briefed him last night."

Her mouth twitched right back at him.

Her nose did, too. That's when she smelled a change on him. Tanner's pheromones were completely different since her last direct encounter with him. He wasn't a "lone" wolf anymore. That's why he had been tasked with delivering her to the witch's home.

"Don't tell me you matched with the la—"

"Everybody needs to shut the fuck up about it," Tanner snapped before pointing his drink in the direction he wanted Iris to walk.

"The witches will heal her," Iris soothed before taking a sip of her coffee. "It's just that the brain is a delicate thing. They have to go slow, and careful. The seizures will start to fade and then they will be gone altogether."

"Turn right," he growled. "Keep walking to the end of the corridor. We don't need to chitchat."

For one second, Iris wished she did have a wolf to push at Tanner—an alpha wolf who could bring the man to heel. She just wasn't sure whether the push would be a gentle nudge or a whack upside the back of his head.

Maybe both. First the whack, then the nudge.

# CHAPTER 15

Knocking twice on a set of massive double doors near the heart of the cave system, Tanner shot a gravelly warning at Iris. "Remember Oscar is a cub, not a con."

Her fingers tingled with the threat of witch light, but Esme opened the door before Iris could succumb to the temptation of zapping the crabby old wolf on the tip of his scarred nose.

Stepping forward, Esme gently cupped Iris's shoulders, kissed her cheek, then repeated the assault on Tanner. He accepted the witch's attention with a stiff body and a look of spreading horror across his face.

"Are you coming in?" Esme asked him.

Tanner shook his head, his reaction a little too exaggerated unless they were entering some kind of plague house. Iris brushed past him, relished the way he recoiled from the contact, then stood quietly staring back at Tanner as Esme shut and locked the doors.

"I guess that leaves you to guard me," Iris said.

Catching the look that crossed the witch's face, she groaned.

"If Cade is here, why can't I smell more than traces of him?"

"He's in a shielded room," Esme explained, leading her down a hallway. "Denver and Oscar are with him. We hold a lot of security meetings here, so the first thing I did was put up an all-points spell in one of the bigger rooms, carve symbols in the rock walls and fill the etchings with silver—among other protective measures. Unless you're the one who did the spelling, it stops all abilities to detect what is on the other side—well, on either side. They are as in the dark about us as you are about them."

Coming to a stop, she gestured at another set of doors. "Here we are."

Iris waited for Esme to open the doors. Instead, the witch lightly curled a hand around Iris's wrist.

"You're trying to read me," Iris said. "I've noticed you touch people when you get stressed about them. Sometimes, you do it to push a calming energy at them. Other times, you're tugging at their thoughts. You're tugging right now. It feels like there are actual strings inside me that you're picking at. Disconcerting at a minimum."

"Sorry," Esme said, quickly withdrawing her hand. "It's a hard habit to control when I'm nervous."

"Well, stop worrying. I've questioned dozens of children while their trauma was fresh. I'm not going to be any less gentle or careful because Oscar is a shifter."

"Oh, I don't think that's my problem," Esme said, her gaze flicking at the double doors. "Not exactly. I think you will tread more carefully than you have with any child before. The energy in the room is bad, though. Denver is here to protect Oscar from you, and Cade is here to protect you from Denver."

Iris barked out a laugh then forced her expression into a stern frown. "Neither of them should be present, they can't help the process, only inhibit it."

Esme finally grabbed the door knob, her sigh escaping as she turned it and the internal bolt slid back. "And yet they are here, and here they shall remain."

The room was so well spelled that opening the door created a small breeze. With it came an odor that turned Iris's stomach.

"What is it?" Esme asked.

Iris brought a hand to her nose, desperately wishing she had the little stick of menthol rub she took to fresh homicide scenes.

"You can't smell it?" she said, slowly moving toward where the scent was strongest. Bypassing Cade, she stopped at the big club chair where Oscar sat on Denver's lap.

The cub looked up and smiled, his teeth like small pearls and his eyes like big, black opals. A beautiful, angelic child.

"Could you take Oscar for a second?" she asked the witch.

Esme complied despite the warning look on her mate's face. When she lifted the cub and started to walk away, the stench followed after her.

"You can give him back," Iris directed. "I'd like to talk to you in the hall again."

"What?" Esme asked once they were alone. "You literally turned green in there."

"There's an odor…something I've smelled once before."

"You've smelled all of them before," Esme snapped, her gaze sharp and worried. "What are you saying?"

"You were spelling Oscar at Cade's home," Iris answered, her brain casting around for explanations. "When I saw the cubs here in the caves, they were on the other side of a thick plate of glass. I can only tell you that, right now, he reeks of something I have only encountered once—the night Hank Mercer tried to kill me. He had two helpers, wolves I'd never met before. They weren't part of our clan. The scent is the same."

For a second, the claim against the cub was forgotten as Esme stared at Iris with a wide, distressed gaze.

"Hank Mercer tried to kill you? Does Cade know?"

"Focus," Iris bit out, immediately wishing she could take back the tone she had used. "Sorry, but what Cade knows isn't relevant now. But, yes, that's why I ran away. That's what you sensed when you said I needed to step the fuck up."

"I didn't say 'fuck,'" the witch whispered, her tender-hearted nature on display as her big green eyes grew luminous with the threat of tears. "And I'm sorry I snapped at you about it. But I feel you are incredibly important to our survival, regardless of whether you are Riya's heir."

Iris forced down the impulse to roll her eyes at the mention of the last All-Mother.

"Look, let's go back in, only spell Oscar as you were before. When I want you to stop, I'll tug my ear."

She demonstrated the gesture. "I want to confirm that the smell goes away when you're spelling him as opposed to something happening to him since he was at Cade's cabin."

Esme frowned. "I've held Oscar today. Shouldn't you smell it on me, too? Shouldn't you have—"

Iris threw her hand up. "I am *not* a wolf, damn it. I smelled Cade while I was still inside the club in Syracuse and he was a good thousand meters away outside. But even if you didn't have these damn doors spelled, my nose wouldn't tell me who was in the room. The stink would be there, though. I know that much."

"You feel that much," Esme corrected, her mouth stuck in a frown. "Maybe it's because you're both a witch and a wolf..."

She trailed off before Iris could tell her to shut up again.

"We'll figure that bit out later," Esme said, then pushed into the room, her lips already moving, the nearly inaudible murmurs clearing the air around her as Oscar started to fall asleep in Denver's arms.

"That's enough," Iris said a few seconds later, forgetting all about the ear tug. Noticing the question burning in Denver's gaze, she butted her chin in his direction. "I'll answer your questions after I've spoken with Oscar."

The cub roused at her use of his name. Lifting his gaze, he offered a disarming smile of recognition. When Iris requested a pen and paper, he charmed both away from her and began filling the first sheet with spiraling, impersonal doodles as she asked him about the day Denver found him.

"I was hungry," he said, pulling tighter to the big wolf holding him. "Denver gave me beef jerky."

"Do you remember who gave you food before Denver?"

The pen froze in his hand, his face going blank for an instant before he shook his head and offered one of his disarming smiles, his black gaze alight with tiny fireflies.

"I think you do remember," she said, placing a hand on Oscar's knee.

Magic flowed from her fingertips, lapping like the ocean tide at the boy's resistance.

Her chest squeezed in recognition at how many times she had used the same trick during homicide investigations. She hadn't been a fool about the wards she carved into her skin or the chants she knew, but she had been blind to using magic as an interrogation technique.

"Don't," Denver growled when he realized what Iris

was doing. The chin that had been smoothly shaven when Iris entered the room now sported half an inch of stubble as he fought to keep his wolf in check.

Cade and Esme rose from where they sat.

"I really need you to leave—" Iris began.

Denver didn't let her finish. He slid Oscar onto the chair and stood, moving so that he loomed over Iris.

"No, you're leaving," he said, each word carefully enunciated as his fangs threatened to erupt. "You can start with the other cubs. Their memories are fresher and they arrived in better health."

Redirecting her attention to Denver, she leaned closer, an almost pleading tone coating her words. "You don't have to leave the room, but the *clan* needs as much space as you can give me. Oscar needs it."

Esme intervened, placed her open palm against Denver's chest and coaxed him toward the furthest corner. Her fingers softly glowed with witch light as the big wolf relented.

Iris turned her attention back to Oscar. Clearly feeling the distance that had been added between him and his fiercest protector, the boy looked up with a glitter of tears swimming in his gaze.

Seeing that broken look, Iris couldn't help but do something she had never done with any other child she had interviewed; she scooped him up then sat down in the chair with him bundled on her lap.

The stench of what he'd been through covered him

like a blanket, but she held him close and put her cheek against his as she spoke.

"We're going to play a game," she said, keeping her tone light despite her stomach curdling inside her body. "I want you to close your eyes and picture the color gray. Then, when I say a word or words, I want you to make a picture of them against the gray. Okay?"

Oscar nodded, his small frame relaxing in her arms and his head lulling back against her shoulder. Iris started easy, saying Denver's name.

"Gold," the boy said, joy lightening his tone.

"That's great," Iris continued, her eyes shut and her mind alert as the gray behind her own eyelids started to fill with Denver's image. Clearly, the cub viewed Denver as a giant because the image crowded the corners of Iris's vision. "How about Denver in his truck?"

A smaller version of Denver appeared, only his head and the top half of his upper chest visible through the vehicle's window. Lifting his hand, a toy fire engine appeared, its metal frame all red and shiny.

"And the first time you rode in Denver's truck, the place where the trip started."

The gray returned, the outline of dark slate bricks and black asphalt the only shapes discernible. The image matched the information in Oscar's file; Denver had found him in an alley on a cold, misty morning.

Oscar trembled against Iris. She wrapped her arms around him a little more tightly and urged warmth into his body in case he was merely remembering the damp chill of that place.

"Before the alley," she prodded.

Pure white, blinding in its brightness, filled her mind, the neurons of her brain momentarily seared.

She slipped into the memory, living it in real time with Oscar as the unbearable brightness eased to show her the antiseptic walls of an operating room.

In the room's center were not one, but two surgical tables. A pregnant woman was strapped down on the first table, her body seemingly nude but for restraints and a sheet that covered from just below the woman's collarbone to her ankles. The other table remained empty, but prepped.

Her mind's eye turning as Oscar's focus shifted, Iris saw the rolling tray between the two tables, its contents covered with a thin, sterile fabric. Carried by someone, Oscar was brought to the empty table. Iris watched as the scared cub—naked, shivering, and flailing—stopped fighting the person carrying him. With terror in his eyes and voice he clung desperately to his captor then, in an effort to stay off the table he could see he was destined to be strapped to like the woman.

The grip on him tightened as a deep, masculine voice told him quietly, "You're going to be my brave boy."

Oscar made a soft squeak of compliance as the man placed him on the steel gurney. The cub looked up, showing Iris a tall man wearing clothing as white as the room and a paper mask over his mouth and nose.

The man had black hair and a dark, volcanic gaze that frightened the boy even further.

The man's pupils were indistinguishable from the irises. And the small veins that should've been red against the white of his eyes were black as tar.

*That's the Bogeyman...*

Oscar wasn't speaking to her in his memory; he was talking to himself, his fearful brain strangling the name before it could escape his lips.

She felt the terror he did as he remembered why it was he knew that name.

Another cub had called the dark man that—once.

No one ever saw the boy again.

# CHAPTER 16

Iris watched as Oscar tried to move off the table, but other men entered the room just then, blocking his escape.

The first man wore clothes like the Bogeyman but colored green. The mask was green, too, with shaded goggles to cover his eyes. The second man was by the pregnant woman's table, standing at the end with his hands alongside her head.

"Place the cub on his stomach," the Bogeyman ordered, removing the fabric covering the tray. Several scalpels and a row of five ametrine crystals were beneath.

Selecting one of the surgical blades, he pulled the sheet from the woman. He balanced the instrument on her naked belly and then used one gloved finger to trace the curve of a smile on the underside of her stomach.

"A shame she doesn't scar each time," he murmured.

"I've lost count of how many pups I've put in or pulled from her belly."

Oscar's stomach clawed its way up to his throat as he instinctively understood the man's intention. He looked away from the woman's torso, focusing instead on her face.

Dark blond tendrils escaped the plastic cap holding her hair in place. She was pretty. Familiar. Without her eyes open, he couldn't be sure, but Oscar was hit with the sense of having seen her once before, remembering her blue-green eyes as clearly as if they were open right now.

The Bogeyman snapped his gaze up at the man behind Oscar. "I said on his stomach!"

Each word was issued slow, precise and louder than the one before it. The way the Bogeyman spoke scared Oscar. Everything he said was in anger. To Iris, he didn't merely sound violent, he sounded fueled, crazed by unmitigated hatred. Of who, she had no idea.

The way he was patting Oscar on the head with his big hand seemed at odds with the way he was speaking.

His eyes matched his voice, though.

*Evil.*

The Bogeyman was pure evil.

Oscar could sense it, just as Iris could.

The assistant flipped Oscar roughly onto his stomach then. All at once, the boy lost the fight to be brave.

The Bogeyman didn't seem to notice or care, his attention now solely on the task at hand. His fingers moved over Oscar's spine, tracing the vertebrae and delivering small pinches to the flesh every other inch.

At the same time, on the opposite table, blue light began to dance in the space between the second man's hands and the pregnant woman's head.

Oscar looked over and saw her eyelids slide open, her sea-green gaze meeting his. The dance of light against her temples intensified as the worker standing beside Oscar wrapped his hands around Oscar's head.

Everything soon dulled. The white room faded, as did the once brilliant ocean hues of the woman's irises. The cold metal and even the dreadful sound of the Bogeyman talking to his assistants became muted. Distant.

Returning back to the woman, the Bogeyman took a scalpel in hand. With the tip of the instrument no more than a millimeter from the woman's flesh, he repeated the shape of the smile he'd traced on her belly earlier, marking the path he was about to cut.

"Time to meet your new baby brother, my boy."

---

EXCRUCIATING PAIN SURGED THROUGH HER BODY AS IRIS released her hold on the now shrieking cub thrashing around on her lap.

She tried to detach from the boy's mind, but her thoughts felt too heavily sedated to manage the feat.

She realized then her entire body had stopped taking

orders from her brain as well, rendering her unable to let go of Oscar has he twisted and flailed in her arms.

Heavy-limbed, helpless, she watched a swift, violent change overtake his small form as he shifted to his wolf form for the first time.

His arms and legs lengthened, his nails sharpening to claws, his teeth to fangs. Hair sprouted along the snout that had replaced his nose.

Howling, Oscar swiped at her face just as Denver scooped the cub up.

Sharp, stabbing pain immediately sliced through the haze, but Iris still couldn't control her movements or her mind. She had ventured too deep into Oscar's consciousness, detaching from her own so thoroughly, her body was slow to recover and reconnect to her own psyche.

Her lips moved with the boy's as he screamed out, still trapped in his memory, his small, sharp-tipped fists pummeling the big wolf's chest.

"No, no, no! You're not my daddy!"

A new, blistering hot burst of pain cut Iris's connection with the cub then as her body began rejecting the silver jewelry embedded in her skin.

Flesh separated to push out the silver, her nipples splitting. Further down, between her thighs, pure, gruesome agony engulfed her.

She dropped onto the floor. Cade shot over to catch her and cushion her fall.

Immediately, Esme swarmed in front of Iris, the witch's attention pulled in two directions at once as Oscar continued to scream and thrash in Denver's hold while Iris howled in pain.

Next to Esme, an arm nearly struck her. The limb, covered in fur the color of iron left to rust, and dark purple paint at the tip of its sharp claws, took another swing at the witch.

The blow again didn't land, because Cade was now restraining her wrist.

*Her wrist.*

Iris could feel Cade squeezing her hand, restraining her without hurting her, his voice and all his energy directed at her. "Calm your wolf, baby," he urged. "Feel me, let my wolf guide you."

She wanted to obey, but couldn't. She continued to struggle against both Cade and Esme, physically and mentally.

Her field of vision shrank away.

Seconds passed as all the voices in the room coalesced into a single buzzing drone, save one. Oscar's shrieks was the only one that had yet to fade. They chased her down the black hole she was falling in, both her mind and body swiftly shutting down, stealing her from her surroundings.

"No! I don't want you to be my daddy!" screeched Oscar, the terror in his voice shattering her heart.

One final memory from Oscar came to her on the tail end of his scream.

*The Bogeyman insisted all the boys call him father.*

And with that final, horrifying thought, she crumpled to a limp, unconscious heap.

# CHAPTER 17

Waking on a bed in strange surroundings, Iris forced her eyelids to open.

Her nose lifted to scent the room while her vision took its sweet time un-blurring. Sensing no immediate danger, she lifted her hand and examined it. Relief swept through her upon seeing the pale, rounded flesh and light dusting of hair so fine it was almost invisible.

With that question answered, she lifted her aching head high enough to look down her body. An uncomfortable image greeted her. A thin white sheet draped her flesh, the fabric's color and weight distressingly similar to what she had witnessed covering the woman in the operating room. Like the woman, she seemed naked as well.

Hesitant fingers plucked at the top edge of the sheet. One of her last memories was of the silver separating from her flesh, slicing at some of her most sensitive areas.

She looked under the cover and a little more tension fled her body.

The silver bars were gone and the nipples appeared to have healed completely. For the moment, she would take it for granted that the flesh from the other piercing was whole, too.

Starting to sit up, she changed direction quickly to clutch at the sheet as she heard movement on the other side of the door. She didn't need to scent the visitor because his wolf pushed ahead of him, entering the room before he twisted the handle and the door swung open.

Cade looked at Iris, his breathing labored and his eyelids fluttering with stunned blinks. Now that he was in the room, he filled her senses. The clean spray of wintergreen and pine tickled her nose while the comforting heat of his wolf wrapped around her bare shoulders.

*Bare shoulders...*

Right, she needed to fix that, especially since Esme and Denver were coming down the hall at full speed, Esme's hand reaching out to jerk Cade by the collar if she managed to get close enough to him.

Sensing them, Cade moved the rest of the way into the room and shut the door, calling over his shoulder for the pair to wait. Turning his attention to Iris, he studied her face. Then his gaze moved lower, a smile playing at the corner of his mouth.

Iris knew the smile, knew he was about to turn insufferable from having been so right for so very long.

"Don't say it," she warned.

Grinning a little wider, Cade shook his head. "The words didn't even cross my mind, baby."

*Yeah, right.*

She rolled her eyes at him and pulled the sheet closer to her body. "I need clothes."

"Not from where I'm standing," he countered and took another step closer to the bed. His wolf reached out, searching for its mate and nuzzling along her neck and shoulder when he found her.

*I'm here*, that annoying voice from the morning gleefully crowed.

"This isn't the time or place for that," Iris growled, no menace in the sound because her wolf refused to ally against her mate.

"You're right," he smirked. "We should go now. We can be at my cabin in half an hour or so."

Great! His hormones were overriding his responsibilities. In some ways, he was still that eighteen-year-old wolfling who had turned her drunk with need whenever he came near.

"Esme," she said, raising her voice just enough to catch the witch's attention on the other side of the door. "Some clothes, please."

That was all the authority Esme needed to barge in. In the short time since Cade had shut her out, she had retrieved a fresh change of clothing in Iris's size.

"Do you need any help?" Esme asked.

Interlacing his fingers, Cade stretched them, the joints popping in relief. "If she does, I'm available."

Iris rolled her eyes in his direction. She would wait until she was dressed to work on his attitude of entitlement. He was crazy if he thought her shifting had solved everything. She didn't care how delicious he smelled or the effect his presence had on her now that the silver was out of her body.

Turning her gaze on Esme, Iris smiled. "Can you get him to give me a few minutes of privacy?"

"My pleasure." Esme waggled her brows and then she rolled her fingers, witch light dancing along their tips.

"Ems..." Caution entered Cade's tone. He'd undoubtedly seen what happened to wolves the witch turned her magic on. He didn't want to be on the receiving end of one of her more aggressive spells. "This is between mates. You know that."

Iris growled. Cade growled back, but with an entirely different intent, one that wasn't appropriate when they had an audience. The vibration continued to roll through his throat, Iris's resolve to make him leave receding.

*Damn that sound was...*

She shook her head. She'd think about what that particular growl of his did to her later, hopefully when she was alone. Right now, she needed clothes. She had to talk to Denver and Esme about what she'd seen inside Oscar's memories.

"Out," Iris ordered. Extending her arm, she pointed at the door. Her entire arm glowed with magic and she pushed her wolf at him.

Cade stumbled backward for an instant then dropped

his head like a bull ready to charge. She abandoned her order, retracting the command but not the request.

"The cubs don't have time for us to argue about this," she soothed. This time, when she pushed her wolf at him, the gesture was a gentle caress of fur on fur.

"Please," she added.

Cade left, his feet dragging with reluctance. Esme followed a few seconds later after Iris said she could manage on her own. With her immediate need for clothing satisfied, she spent a few seconds taking stock of her body. Her muscles were stiff and her mouth felt gluey, as if she'd spent a full day knocked out.

A glance at the clock next to the bed confirmed that at least several hours had passed.

Running a hand through her hair, she opened the bedroom door to find Cade, Denver and Esme standing in the hall. Denver flashed from barely holding back in confronting her while she remained in the bedroom to full in her face, his topaz gaze boring into her skull.

"What did you do to him?" he barked at Iris, concern for Oscar warring with aggression in his voice.

Esme and Cade moved immediately to intervene, the witch calming while Cade was anything but. He stepped forward, bristling, snarling a warning at Denver.

Iris slid a hand onto Cade's shoulder and lightly squeezed. It was the first time she had touched him since she had shifted and the realization threatened to smash the calm facade she projected to dust.

Forcing her attention back to the angry shifter looming over her, she managed a smile.

Before yesterday, she'd only had her own will and her magic to push Denver back.

*Now? If he didn't stop coming at her, the jerk wouldn't know what hit him.*

# CHAPTER 18

Chuckling over her wolf's sass and strength, Iris let her rise up to greet the clan leader, barely filtered, and cloaked in all the power of her magic.

Denver's gaze remained as hard as yellow diamonds, but she saw his wolf blink. Just a little, but it was enough. Easing back, she stopped the amusement that had continued seeping up her throat, not wanting to be overtly disrespectful.

She dipped her head then, acknowledging Denver's status as clan leader, before pointing toward the living room visible at the end of the hall.

Denver led the way, Esme behind him. With his palm intimately placed against the small of Iris's back, Cade guided her forward.

"I think that's a first for him since he fully came into his wolf," Cade whispered into her ear.

Iris pushed down a victorious whoop.

She needed to work with Denver instead of having him constantly fight her at every turn. She also wanted to remain friends with his tenderhearted mate.

Entering the front room, Iris looked at Esme first. Kindness danced in the witch's gaze and she threw Iris a discreet wink.

Relieved, Iris sank onto the couch. Cade slid next to her. Out of sight of Esme and Denver, he gave her flesh a reassuring squeeze.

"Well?" Denver prompted.

His expression didn't look like he was ready to listen. Iris mashed her lips together as she weighed how much information she should parcel out at the moment. Deciding she would have to decide detail by detail and judge by everyone's reaction on how much more to reveal, she began.

"Oscar's last memory from before he was discovered by Denver was an operating room."

That hooked Denver's attention immediately. "Was he hurt?"

She shook her head then drew a deep breath. "Nothing seemed to be wrong with him. There was a woman in the room...pregnant..."

Her gaze jumped to Esme, recognition punching Iris in the throat. Words jumped from her before she had a chance to consider whether she should hold the information back. "Her face and eyes were an exact match for yours, but she had a wolf's physique."

Esme's face went slack before her expression sharpened. "What do you mean?"

"A twin—" Iris started.

Their reactions identical and simultaneous, Esme and Denver each shook their head, dismissing the idea. They both spoke, their words overlapping with the same message.

"There has never been a birth of twins, let alone one wolf and the other not."

Iris shrugged. "And, outside of The Nakari, I'm the first wolf to cast—that anyone knows of."

Cade pushed a little closer to Iris at her admission. Warmth flooded her chest, but she forced herself to ignore the sensation for the moment. She needed time to figure out what it meant to be both and what it meant for any possible future between her and Cade.

"So the woman looked like Esme and she was pregnant," Denver countered, his tongue stalling on the final word. Leaning closer to his mate, he curled his arm behind her, his hand resting on her opposite hip. He pushed his nose against her hair and then his lips pressed against her cheek.

Casting an apologetic look at the witch, Iris continued. "There were three men in the room, but one was clearly in charge. He referred to Oscar as 'my boy' and he had the same coloring, jet black hair and eyes—"

"Are you saying the man was a shifter?" Cade asked.

"No," Iris answered, her gaze still on Esme. The witch seemed to take a long time processing the information, her body physically backing away from some realization she didn't want to accept.

"I think she's describing Quentin," Esme said after a few more seconds of deliberation. "I've recognized the physical similarities, so has Lana, but we keep telling ourselves it's coincidental, that the coloring of all the cubs is—"

"Stop," Denver interrupted. He softened his sharp denial a second later as he nuzzled Esme's cheek once more. "Baby, Seth and I saw that bastard just as clearly as you and Lana did. We both thought on this and dismissed the possibility."

Esme looked away from her mate, the gears in her head still chewing at the issue until she finally found the answer. "The discovery of the cubs has brought so much hope to the clan. Everyone immediately falls in love with them. So why would we notice the impossible when we don't want to? Quentin isn't a wolf, he couldn't father Oscar, at least not naturally."

Forgetting her earlier desire to proceed with caution, Iris decided to throw a little kerosene onto the conversation. "You've already theorized that at least some Hunters are basically latents—the source of their magic the same as female latents. Could one be capable of impregnating a female shifter? And, as a latent, Camille could have gotten pregnant by a shifter, had twins and..."

All the air seemed to leave the room at what Iris was about to suggest, the tension broken only by Denver renewing his disbelief.

"We only have a cub's memory," he said. "Not even that, really, just what you thought he experienced."

"Iris has never seen Quentin," Cade reminded them.

"That's true," Iris agreed, glad that Cade was there to plug the gaps in her claims. Leaning forward, she focused her attention on Denver, her mind examining Oscar's memories for a detail that might convince the big wolf in front of her, or at least ease his conceding to her arguments.

"When you picked Oscar up as he was shifting," Iris began, her heart starting to knock around in her chest as she realized what she was about to say could tip Denver's opinion solidly against her. "He was screaming, 'You're not my daddy' and then 'I don't want you to be my daddy.' Do you remember?"

The look on Denver's face told Iris that he would never forget those words. Misunderstood, they had stabbed him in the heart.

Softly pushing her wolf at him, she tried to ease his heartache. "Those words weren't directed at you. They were for the black-haired man in charge."

There—she saw it, a crack in Denver's resistance. Now if she could just pry it open a little more instead of saying something that would seal the crack forever. She hesitated, thinking it through, what each detail she had seen meant and how accepting of those details Denver and Esme would be.

"Don't hold back," the witch whispered.

She had remained motionless since her last question,

her gaze locked on her hands as they twisted in her lap. She held herself slightly apart from her mate despite his attempts to pull her close and ease the pain from the conversation's repeated reminders that she had not yet conceived his child when so many other latents had become pregnant from the first time they joined with their mate.

Giving a nervous lick of her lips, Iris pushed forward. "The man placed Oscar on a second operating table. Between the two tables, there was a tray loaded with scalpels and ametrine crystals, each about as big as the tip of my thumb."

That caught Esme's attention. Blood drained from her face and she shook her head.

"I didn't see what was done with the crystals," she assured Esme and Denver. "But the man seemed to be measuring the spaces between Oscar's vertebrae and then he picked up the scalpel and turned to the woman..."

Unsure of how she could possibly tell them the last detail, Iris drew a deep breath. They had to know and she had to tell them, no matter how much the visions had made her gut clench and threaten to spew.

Cade pressed against her back, his thumb gently stroking her flesh in a gesture of support. At least she hoped it was support. It felt amazing to know she wasn't alone any longer and that she hadn't permanently pushed him away.

Ignoring the urge not to, Iris met Esme's gaze. She saw a flash of fear, but also forgiveness and friendship.

Drawing strength from Cade and the witch, she pushed the words out, praying Denver would at least turn them over in his mind before rejecting their validity.

"The last thing the man said before Oscar pulled back from the memory was that it was time for Oscar to meet his baby brother."

# CHAPTER 19

*e sang du bébé...*"

"L Esme's hands curled around the edge of the cushion beneath her. She swayed, her body remaining upright only because of her mate's quick response.

Folding his arms around Esme, Denver closed his eyes as he curled his wolf protectively against her.

Across from them, Iris and Cade waited for Esme to recover and explain the term.

"It's the worst kind of magic," she whispered after a few seconds. Tears flowed freely down her rounded cheeks and her hands slid across her stomach to protectively clutch at her sides. "A sacrifice of absolute purity is needed. But the magic produced is nearly unbreakable, if it can even be detected."

"So whatever Quentin was going to do to Oscar, he needed a sacrifice." Iris said, her memory straining for any other information Oscar's mind might have imparted before the revived trauma forced his first shift into his wolf. "What about the crystals?"

Esme shook her head. "Witches have been using crystals containing silver or iron for millennia. They act as magnifiers and I think my mother may have found a way to use them almost like a radio."

"You need to examine Oscar—" Iris started.

Surprisingly, Esme objected first. "He won't let me touch him since the interview."

Thick tears spilled from the witch's eyes. The strain in her relationship with the cub had been slowly building, starting with Oscar's first encounter with Iris, when he had responded to her wolf even as she denied her nature.

From that point on, he had gravitated toward the pregnant latents and she-wolves while squirming away from Esme's embrace.

"It's because of the woman on the table," Iris suggested.

"Not all of it," Esme whispered. "And I've had more than half a year to find something wrong with..."

Still mindful of her mate's fierce affection for the cub, she trailed off, her eyes darting to the side for a moment before she met Iris's gaze once more. "You'll need to examine him. If he'll let you. You have the best chance of detecting anything. You already smelled the magic on him."

Denver moved restlessly where he sat. Iris expected

him to veto the idea, but he rose after a few seconds and gestured that she should follow him.

He passed through a door opposite the hall through which they had entered the living room, Iris close on his heels and Cade and Esme behind her.

Halfway down the hall, Denver stopped and stood in front of a door, but didn't move to open it.

"There are other cubs in there with him," Iris said, a wave of nausea rolling over her at the smell.

"Two others," Esme agreed. "I was watching them before I sensed you waking up."

Denver stepped out of the way, flicked his hand at Iris for her to enter. Opening the door, she saw all three cubs sitting on top of the bed. Oscar had a red fire truck centered on his lap, but he and the other cubs held hands so that their arms formed a loose circle.

Seeing Iris, Oscar slid his hands onto the fire truck, one finger absently flicking at the toy's ladder. More vehicles were scattered on the bed and the other cubs started playing with them.

Esme gestured at the visiting children. "Micah, Adam...help me make lunch."

"Up," Denver ordered when the boys didn't budge. "You can play some more after you eat."

Micah and Adam rose, their feet shuffling along the carpet in unwilling obedience. Before they could reach the door, Cade stopped them. Lifting one brow as he stared at Iris, Cade poked his chin in the smaller cub's direction.

Smiling at the boy despite the smell of dark magic on

him and his playmate, Iris ran a hand against his spine as she asked, "What's your name, sweetie?"

"Adam," he mumbled. "Did you send Oscar back to the bad man?"

Guilt clouding her gaze, she shook her head. "Oscar hasn't gone anywhere, he just had a very bad dream."

She turned to the other boy and rested her palm between his shoulder blades. "You must be Micah."

A frown pulled at the corners of her mouth and she sucked a deep breath in. Glancing at Esme, she offered a discreet nod before breaking contact with Micah. "You two run along and help Esme with lunch."

She waited for them to leave before she turned to Oscar. He had climbed up into Denver's arms, his small hands clasped behind the big wolf's neck.

Seeing Iris approach, he buried his face against Denver's chest.

"Honey, I just want to make sure you are okay." She placed her hand on his back, watched him arch his spine in an attempt to avoid contact. "Maybe we can talk after lunch?"

Face still buried against Denver, Oscar shook his head.

"Okay, baby." She rubbed her hand against his back, pushing a sleepy magic through her fingertips to calm him. "We'll wait until you're ready."

Iris retreated into the hall, Cade by her side. He closed the door to Oscar's room, hesitated a second then wrapped his arms around her.

"All of them?" he asked.

She nodded, the sob breaking from her throat muffled by his clothes and chest. Her arms around his waist, she squeezed hard, trying not to think about the number of cubs that might have crystals in them, the terrible but unknown "why" of it fading in importance as she tallied the number of infants Quentin might have slaughtered in order to place those crystals.

Bile rose in her throat, acidic and uncontrollable. Cade guided her into a bathroom and stood beside her, holding Iris's hair as she spilled her guts into the toilet.

When she finished, he filled a rinse cup with water from the sink and handed it to her. He sat on the edge of the tub, waiting until she finished before he pulled her onto his lap and held her once more.

"Shh..." he soothed. "It's done. We need to focus on stopping it from ever happening again."

She nodded, unable to dam her tears and wishing like hell she could reach through Oscar's memories and shred the black-haired man into ribbons.

# Chapter 20

"Did you notice how the cubs were holding hands when we entered the room?" Cade asked as the adults regrouped after Denver finished comforting Oscar.

"They hold hands like that a lot," Esme answered. "We figured they were all bonding so very closely because they sensed how much their circumstances were alike."

Magic leaked from the witch, her tears tinged blue after she had verified Iris's findings on Adam and Micah once she knew what to search for. A nervous energy vibrated in the air around her, humming soft but deadly in its intensity.

"I think I know," Cade said. His chest tightened, cutting off the air he needed to explain. Meeting Denver's hard stare, he saw understanding slowly dawn in the other man's gaze.

"It's a signal boost," Denver answered, all the blood

draining from his face so that the topaz eyes burned against his pale skin like the sun at high noon. "They could use it to find the clan. Whatever the purpose of the crystals, it's why the cubs are still safe when we find them and why the Hunters have never ambushed us while we retrieved the boys. They want them with us and watch over them until we arrive and take the boys away."

Iris sagged against Cade. Feeling his arm circle her shoulders and the soft nuzzle of his wolf, she closed her eyes and pressed her face against his neck.

"Can we take the crystals out?" Denver asked.

Everyone looked at Esme for the answer. Aware of the attention focused on her, she stared at the ground and slowly shook her head.

"I don't think so," she went on after a long moment. "Especially in the cubs who haven't shifted yet—their healing isn't as accelerated. We need more healers than we have and we could paralyze them. Hit the wrong spot on their spinal cord and their body will shut down."

Her hands twisted against one another, magic sparking from the tips.

"And that is without addressing what protective spells Quentin has placed on the crystals. If he sacrificed pure magic to place the crystals and keep them undetected, it may take an equal sacrifice to get them out."

Esme stopped talking, her lips remaining slightly parted as she took shallow breaths and her skin turned milky white.

"Baby..." Denver cradled his mate's face, his lips

lightly dusting one cheek before he forced her gaze up to meet his. "I need you to hold it together, love. You have to feel a little less. Can you do that? For Oscar and all the other boys?"

He kissed her lips, kissed her tears. She nodded but her expression remained unconvinced.

"We have to disperse the cubs," Denver said, still holding Esme but directing his words at Cade. "Off clan lands, no cubs together, and with as many wolves and charms protecting each boy as we can spare."

Standing, Cade pulled his cell phone out. "I'll call Oram and get the West Virginia wolves mobilized."

Pausing, he looked at Iris, his gaze asking permission to leave her alone for a few minutes or longer despite the grief visible on her face.

She nodded. "I'll stay with Esme while you and Denver make your calls."

Slower to leave his mate, Denver stood, his hands lingering around Esme's tear-stained face.

"I'm okay," the witch sniffed. She pointed her chin in Iris's direction. "We can try to come up with some solutions while you're on the phone with the other clan leaders."

She drew a breath in, her hesitation stalling Denver a few more seconds before she added, "I need to discuss this with the rest of the Witches' Council."

Iris watched as Denver's expression slowly changed from tender to something only slightly less pliant than steel. "After I've talked to the other clan leaders."

Esme offered a small blink of acquiescence, the downward curve of her mouth indicating that she would only keep the information from the Council for a short time.

Satisfied, Denver followed Cade from the room. Esme immediately moved from the couch to sit by Iris. She wrapped her fingers around those of the she-wolf and gazed into Iris's eyes.

"I need you to do something for me before they get back."

Iris swallowed a small lump in her throat, relatively certain what Esme wanted her to do. "Check for crystals?"

"Yes," Esme agreed with a whisper. Releasing her grip on Iris, she turned and presented her back to the she-wolf. "I'm assuming I don't reek, but if the crystals have been with me since childhood..."

"Right. It could be because you're not a wolf. Or the odor could fade with time, with your mother spelling you while the scent would have been detectible. It could also be a matter of intent in the placement."

"To include whether any of the crystals have wards carved in them," Esme agreed. "Were you able to see the crystals clearly enough in Oscar's memory?"

"No," Iris answered as she ran her hands down Esme's spine, starting high and working toward the waist. Reaching the middle, she hesitated.

"Anything?"

Iris felt the quiver in Esme's voice stab at her own chest. The witch was afraid of being betrayed by her own body—a feeling Iris knew all too well. For Esme, it was a new fear, its grip tighter than any vise because of the novelty.

"Not on your spine," Iris answered. Her hands spread farther apart, encompassing the witch's broad hips for a moment before she leaned closer and placed her palms against Esme's lower stomach.

"No," Esme said, her voice so soft that only Iris's wolf could make sense of the sound. "Not there—"

"I'm sorry, sweetie." Iris choked the words out. "I wish—"

Esme shook her head, the thick wavy strands bouncing violently. She placed her hands over Iris's, her energy seeking out the objects the she-wolf had detected. "Why would they do that?"

"Maybe because you're the most powerful witch—"

Another hard shake, blonde curls flying in every direction. "Not anymore. You are, at least once you're properly trained."

Moving down the couch, Esme wiped at her tears and drew a ragged breath in. "I have to get this under control, I can't have Denver distracted by my feelings."

Iris closed the distance between them and wrapped an arm around Esme. "He's your mate," she whispered in the witch's ear. "You're never going to be able to hide your feelings from him. And you shouldn't try. He loves you on a deeply crazy level..."

A small hiccup interrupted the smile forming on Esme's lips. She gave another sniff and nodded before peeking at Iris from beneath lashes still wet with tears.

"Just like Cade is crazy about you."

Iris held her hand up, the fingers splayed for emphasis.

"Slow down, witch," she said with a lighthearted tenderness that stretched Esme's smile a little wider. "Maybe when we have a handle on this cub situation—"

"Nuh-uh." Capturing Iris's hand, Esme wove her fingers through the she-wolf's and softly tugged. "Mates draw strength from one another. We're stronger together. That's one thing I don't think the Hunters have counted on because they turn on each other at the first sign of danger. And with all the latents we've discovered, there are more mates now than..."

Esme tightened her grip on Iris. The witch's lips and brows moved as if she hadn't stopped talking. Her head tilted to the side, and then she gave it a slight shake before her brows knitted.

"What's going on in that head of yours?" Iris asked. "Because it appears to be really entertaining and I could use a laugh right about now."

Esme chewed at her bottom lip a few more seconds before she nodded. "We need to check some of the other latents to make sure they aren't carrying any crystals, but I don't think they will be. They don't come to us at all like the cubs. They remember their families and childhood."

"Okay, I agree we need to check them, but what..." Iris stopped and twirled a few circles with one finger in front of Esme's face. "Was that all about?"

"Maybe nothing," Esme admitted. "But I feel like it's

really important the Hunters haven't picked up on how much strength we gain every time we find another latent. Both from having mated pairs and the extra magic the women bring. Lana took straight to casting and healing and so have some of the others. A few even worked carnivals as psychics."

Releasing her hold on Iris, the witch stood and stared at the door through which Denver and Cade had left. Her hands found her ample hips and her right foot stamped the ground once as she blew a hot puff of air.

"I really need to convene the Witches' Council."

"We need a little more time," Iris said, patting the cushion next to her to draw Esme back to the couch.

"We?" Esme asked, one dark blond brow arching toward the ceiling.

"You and me," Iris snorted. "Not the clan, if you thought that's what I meant. I know wolves have a hard time trusting anyone who can wield magic, more so now that we've learned that Hunters have been using it against us."

"Okay." Esme plopped down next to Iris. "Why do 'we' need more time before I talk to the Witches' Council?"

"For starters, to check a few of the latents, like you suggested." Iris twisted her hands together, the motion audible from how roughly she rubbed. Fighting the urge to light up one of her fingertips with witch light and carve a fresh ward into her skin, she shoved a hand under each armpit.

"Okay," Esme joked, one finger twirling a circle just as Iris had done a few minutes before. "You want to tell me what that's all about? And, for the record, it's not entertaining. I'm stressed as hell!"

Trying to shape an explanation, Iris bounced lightly against the back cushion. "I've been gone twelve years..."

Flooded with the threat of tears, she buried her face in her hands, her elbows propped against the top of her thighs. She felt the soft drape of Esme's arm across her back and then the warm push of the witch's breath against her hair.

She lifted her head for a second, but the room was a blur of tears and she retreated. "I have a few weeks, starting with the attack, that I can barely remember. I would say I can't remember any of it at all, but there are these little flashes, bits and bobs of nightmares that are always the same."

Her hands dropped to her stomach, her arms protectively curling around her flesh. Her chest ached as if a fiery blade had been buried deep inside and still smoldered.

"I've tried to see into your memories," Esme confessed. "But your walls are too thick for a gentle poking around."

Iris turned toward the witch and allowed Esme to wrap her in a gentle embrace. The image of little Oscar in Denver's arms flashed through her head and then she buried her face against Esme's shoulder.

Voice muffled by the witch's flesh, Iris finally found

the strength to make the request that had weighed on her mind since she interviewed the cubs.

"I need you to poke harder, to find out exactly what happened the day I left the clan and those few weeks after," she whispered as Esme soothingly stroked her hair and cooed comforting words of nonsense.

With her body knotting even tighter, she pushed the last words out, uncertain which way they would fall until they passed her lips.

"And I want Cade there when you do it."

# CHAPTER 21

"What's this?" Iris asked as Cade slid a key into a lock on a double set of doors only slightly less impressive than those fronting the Gladwins' living quarters.

"Your new home," he answered, pushing the doors open and guiding her inside.

She stepped in, nose lifting to scent the air.

"If it's my new home, how come I can smell you all over the place?"

Crossing the threshold, he shrugged. "It's were I lived for a few weeks before I moved to the border house. They didn't install anyone new since then."

He swept his arms wide. "Living room."

He pointed at a set of swinging doors next. "Dining room and the kitchen beyond that."

"Are there a set of Chinese menus stuck to the refrigerator with a magnet? Because that's how I cook."

Cade grinned and braced for a slug.

"You'll learn."

Spinning away before she could actually hit him, he turned down a side hall, a finger flicking the doors as he passed them. "Hall bath, office one, office two, bedroom, and...master bedroom."

On that last room, he opened the door and slid inside, leaving Iris to follow him.

She did.

The sheets were still in a tangle, his scent soaked into every surface.

His scent...and only his scent.

Grabbing Iris by the hips, he gently swung her to the edge of the bed and pushed her down until she was sitting, her neck arched to look up at him.

"When I said I wanted someplace private to talk," Iris protested, half-jokingly "I didn't mean your bedroom."

"I said master bedroom," he corrected, dark gaze sparkling at her as he settled against the dresser. His strong hands curled around its top lip and then he nodded. "So, what is it you want to talk about?"

Iris would have preferred the diversion of an argument, especially given the location. She could smell several days' worth of Cade's scent layered around the bedroom. While the mint and pine odors that clung to his presence usually made her crisp-minded, a third odor, one of fresh grass dipped in dew, seemed to inhabit his sleeping area.

Right where her body perched, the scent of mint and pine curled around her thighs like thick fingers.

*Keep it together, North!*

Cade leaned forward, his ass still against the dresser, but his height sufficient that he loomed over her from two feet away. "Baby, everything's about to turn into mobilization central around here. So what did you want to tell me?"

Her mouth flattened. Even though the threat had been present since the beginning of Oscar's rescue, time was still of the essence.

She should just cut to the chase and tell him what he wanted, not deflect the issue by talking about things he already knew—Esme's crystals, how the handful of other latents she and the witch had checked were clear, or how Seth's pack was preparing to take Lana and the Wonder Twins to the West Virginia and Tennessee clans to check their latents.

Or maybe she shouldn't say anything at all. Maybe she shouldn't have him present when Esme and Lana worked on restoring Iris's lost weeks.

"Iris..." Cade eased his way onto the bed next to her, his tone a jumble of frustration, tenderness and impatience.

She drew a shaky breath. He had every right to be impatient. She had made him wait for twelve years.

His hand curled around hers then and she released the breath she had been holding.

Start small, she thought.

"Esme and Lana are going to regress my memory this afternoon."

His gaze widened and he gave a small nod. "I wondered why she didn't argue with Denver about delaying a while longer before convening the Witches' Council."

"Exactly," Iris answered. "That and making sure the other latents in this clan are clear."

"Yeah." A harsh laugh punctuated his agreement as his mind turned toward the crystals in Esme. "We will find Camille one of these days and she better hope someone other than Denver gets to her first."

Pulling Iris's hand onto his lap, Cade tilted his head down so he could see her face and she could see his. He waited for her to say something more. She let him wait, her brain still turning over which was the wiser course— have him present or lie and say that was all she wanted to tell him.

Hell, "wise" wasn't even part of her calculations. She wanted what was less painful for both of them. Only she hurt at the idea of him being absent during the regression every bit as much as his being present cut at her.

Different pains, but equal.

Smothering both was the fear of the unknown. What would she remember? What horrible, terrifying things would come out of her mouth?

"I suppose you don't want me there when it happens?" He said at last.

She didn't listen to the words so much as their tone, at

the fierce quiver of need to protect her and at the under-current of hurt because he thought she didn't want him with her.

She turned toward him, unsheddable tears filling her eyes as she shook her head.

"I absolutely want you with me when they do it."

There! The decision was made; no turning back now.

So why didn't she feel any relief?

# CHAPTER 22

Iris melted into Cade's embrace as he pulled her in close, his big hands soothing and stroking her back. "I didn't think you'd want me there."

A silent, slightly hysterical laugh rang inside her head. She hadn't felt relief over her decision made because so much could still go wrong.

For starters, she could hear what he was asking even though he was holding back—he wanted to know *why* she wanted him there. A simple enough question...which would lead to more questions.

*One step at a time.*

More than one answer to his question came to mind. She felt afraid. Scared shitless, really. And vulnerable. Wholly unable to protect herself during the process.

Cade could keep her safe. And if she shifted again, just as she had done while trapped in Oscar's memories, somebody had to be there to protect Esme and Lana.

"I don't want to repeat what I remember," she answered flatly.

Cade made a little noise at the back of his throat, as if he wanted to call her on the bullshit she'd just spread out in front of him. Instead, he pressed his lips against her hair, nuzzling her for a second before he asked, "Is that all?"

No, but she didn't think she could admit it, not with him sitting so close, his arm already around her, his lips a centimeter from her face.

Letting go of the hand he still held, Cade smoothed his palm across Iris's stomach so that he had her fully encircled in his arms. The kiss he had pressed to her hair moved down to her cheek, his lips whispering over her skin in a feathering of kisses inexorably aimed at her mouth.

She wanted to turn into him, to offer up her submission, to tell him that she wanted him there because she loved him, always had, and was terrified to go in alone.

But she knew where that would lead.

Hell, she was sitting where that would lead!

Pushing lightly at his chest, she cleared a little distance between them. "We can't be intimate...before..."

She wasn't sure about after, either, and Cade knew it. He lifted his dark brows at her, his mouth lightly upturned in a mischievous smile.

"Is that a magic rule, baby?"

"No." She rolled her eyes at him before turning serious. "You might regret it after you hear what I—"

"Never," he interrupted and pulled her close again, his arms tensing as if to ensure she stayed within his embrace. "You're just looking for another excuse to hide, baby. You don't ever need to hide from me again."

His teeth captured the lobe of her ear as one hand slid up the swell of her stomach. Reaching her breast, he paused, the heat of his open palm penetrating her blouse and bra as he gently chewed along the curve of her jaw.

Iris turned her face toward Cade's. His mouth captured hers as his palm slid further up to cup her swollen flesh. His thumb and index finger found the jut of her excited nipple. He gave a slow tug.

"Cade..." She repeated his name in a half-concealed moan, the jaws of her wolf locked around any protest Iris might offer.

He eased off the bed, his tongue and lips unceasing in their sweet torment as his hands gripped her knees and teased her legs apart.

The clothes she had dressed in after shifting were Esme's. Given the fact that she normally wore pants for work, the long, flowing black skirt made her feel partly naked. It didn't help that Esme was so much shorter than Iris.

The hem that usually swished around the witch's ankles fell mid-calf on Iris.

Which meant Cade was able to push the fabric up to her thighs all that much quicker, his touch hotter than lava as his fingertips and palms flowed over her skin.

With one hand against the center of Iris's chest, Cade

coaxed her onto her back, her plump bottom perched at the edge of the mattress and her legs spread as wide as they would go.

Knowing he was seconds from tasting her, Iris felt the first stab of panic and reached for the mass of dark curls slowly descending toward her sex.

Cade let Iris knot her fingers in his hair, but didn't alter his trajectory. When she lightly tried to pull him away, he shook his head. His lips played over her inside thigh, the kisses hotter than his hands had been seconds before.

"Baby, you don't understand what a well-behaved wolf I've been," he cautioned. "You're still in heat."

Kissing her other thigh, Cade let the words sink in. Both relief and regret flooded her. Their one time together hadn't resulted in a pregnancy.

He shushed her as she tensed up. Then he gave a small nip, just hard enough to flush her pale skin without breaking its surface.

"Baby, we haven't had enough time together to change your pheromones," he pressed. "You're still a walking land mine."

Her grip slowly relaxed as she realized his point before he said it.

Cade nipped her again, a little harder and through the thin material of her underwear. "Because of this."

*This—her heat, her soaking wet pussy, the thin layer of perspiration clinging to her body, rich with the scent of a female alpha wolf.*

A harsh, possessive growl vibrated against her thigh, followed by the shriek of fabric as he tore the panties away. Knowing that his gaze was focused on her jumping, squeezing sex, Iris tensed.

"Love, I don't care how many times these have been through the wash, they still have *his* scent buried in them."

*His...*

Esme's skirt, Esme's bra and blouse, Esme's panties carrying traces of Denver's presence while Iris was in heat. Too much for an alpha wolf like Cade to bear, especially with a runaway mate.

She lifted her mound toward his waiting mouth and found a little more stretch to widen her quivering thighs.

She heard him sigh as he lowered his head to taste her, his pace kept slow and sweet the first few seconds. His tongue slid against her clit. His thumbs lightly massaged the perimeter of her pussy.

Their mutual arousal cranked up to full-blown lust, draping over them like an all-consuming blanket.

Gentle licks turned to a rough gnawing of his lips against her flesh, his thick thumbs penetrating her sex as she rocked against his mouth, groaning her need for him to explore deeper.

Her wolf curled low in Iris's gut, reaching out to lick at her mate. Deep growls emanated from Cade's throat, his lips throttling Iris's clit as he pushed three fingers inside her. His palm crowded the exterior of her gate and then he flexed.

Weaving her fingers in his hair, Iris urged Cade closer, wanting his cock in her as she swayed haphazardly at the edge of release. Fire flared through her limbs. Only the dominance of her wolf over her magic kept witch light from erupting around her.

Hips slamming upward, she cried out Cade's name. Looping his free arm beneath her bottom and placing his hand across Iris's mound to hold her down, he dropped his head a few inches.

Tongue replaced fingers. He licked slowly inside her core. Splaying the fingers of the hand over Iris's mound, he found her clit once more with his thick thumb.

Stroking above while licking deep into the center, he began to dominate Iris further below. The jealous star of her ass yielded slowly to one finger, then two.

She howled, her body in a fever pitch, bucking against his face, wetting him with a flood of her juices as she came. She released her stranglehold on his head and wrapped her fingers around the edge of the mattress.

Her nails stabbed at the bedding, witch light dancing at their tips and threatening to ignite the material as she climaxed again.

With a final roll and pitch, she came to a stop, gently squirming against his touch, mewling like a cat instead of the she-wolf she was.

"Don't worry, love," he said, breaking contact with her. "I'm not even close to done with this sweet pussy."

She had less than a second to process Cade's wicked

grin before he flipped her onto her stomach and pushed the skirt up over her ass.

A firm spank startled her.

The muscles of her sex tightened as Cade simultaneously pushed in. Another pulsing second and then he ballooned inside her.

Iris screamed into the mattress as pleasure overloaded her senses. She felt the weight of his chest against her back, his hands knotting in her hair and then twisting so that she turned toward his face.

He thrust his tongue into her mouth, the cream she had released for him coating her taste buds.

Cade kissed like he fucked, rough and demanding one minute, gently circling the next so that she rode a roller coaster of too much and not enough.

"You're never getting away from me again," he warned, his wolf holding her down as he took what was his—what had always been his. "I'm yours for as long as I live and then I'm coming back to haunt you, baby."

Iris moaned, wondering during the interval between heartbeats how Cade had maintained the capacity for speech when she had utterly lost hers. She lifted against him, pussy and thighs squeezing to magnify the already overwhelming size of his cock and the wolf knot at its base.

Cade growled and she knew he wrestled with the need to release.

"No, love." He straightened, finding a hidden reserve

of control she didn't possess. "Not until I hear you howl my name again."

His hands took ownership of her ass, the palms and fingers on the outside, roughly manipulating the full flesh, as both thumbs gently teased the other hole open.

"Howling my name," he repeated, stretching her pussy and ass, rolling and diving until he had her panting for just enough air to remain conscious. "Admitting once and for all that you are my mate."

"Yes." Her high-pitched whine begged him to take her over the edge a second time and finish claiming her with his own climax. "Your mate..."

"You're only halfway there, baby." Cade chuckled, his motions slowing.

*Wrong, wrong, wrong.*

She was all the way there, her tongue frozen as she jerked beneath him, both holes jerking and sucking, drawing him deeper, savoring that final burst of inflation before his cock unleashed inside her.

*"Cade..."* His name erupted from her, starting as a trembling howl that morphed into a breathless moan as pleasure expanded and simply shattered into a kaleidoscope of bliss.

## CHAPTER 23

Two hours later, freshly showered with a towel wrapped around her ample flesh, Iris opened the door of the master bathroom just a crack to find Lana standing at the foot of the bed, a friendly smirk lighting the woman's face.

"I'm glad that's settled," she teased.

Blushing, Iris walked to the dresser where someone had placed a large, unopened box with an all too familiar, smiling logo on it next to a second, used box, its top folded instead of taped.

"We ordered you some undergarments as soon as you arrived, but there's no same or next day delivery out here." Pointing at the used box, she continued. "We also have some first-class seamstresses. They took your measurements from the clothes you were wearing when you came in. When you have a little free time, I can take you to them and you can put an order in."

Iris opened her mouth, couldn't find the words for the gratitude she wanted to express.

"There's no money out here," pausing, Lana snorted. "Well, of course there is but it's mostly all about bartering. Some people sew, some heal and cast, some protect, some hunt and farm...plus, everyone wants Cade a little more mellow. That doesn't happen when you're wearing borrowed panties."

Winking, she stood and walked to the door.

"I'll wait for you in the living room," she said. "When you're finished, I'll escort you to the healing suite where Cade and Esme are waiting."

"I'll just be a few seconds," Iris nodded. With the latent out of the room, she quickly dressed. The need to add new wards to her flesh itched just below the surface, begging her to start with just a scratch or two.

She shook off the urge, the promise she had made to herself and Cade before he left her to shower repeating in her mind.

*No more hiding—not from her mate and not from her past.*

Hair still damp, Iris joined Lana. The latent looped her arm through Iris's, her touch warm with a calming magic.

"Let's put an end to this mystery," she said, her gentle manner coaxing Iris out of the apartment.

THE HEALING SUITE LANA DELIVERED IRIS TO WAS LIKE A pill-shaped cocoon with crystals and silver embedded in its walls.

A chaise covered in freshly laundered blankets centered the room. Around the chaise were three stools, one on each long side and one behind the slightly raised back.

Cade waited at the suite's door, opening it for them as they approached. Lana led the way inside, lightly tugging Iris with her as Cade placed a warm hand against the she-wolf's back to ease her forward.

Didn't they understand how heavy her feet had become or how thick and impossible the air had turned?

"I'm with you, baby," Cade whispered to Iris. "Nothing will ever change that."

Her head dipped in acknowledgment, but she only half believed him. She could have done something in those missing weeks that would turn him away, or have had something done to her that would equally repel him.

Twelve years had passed to weaken the bond between them.

For all she knew, the remaining link was made of little more than air and memories that needed only the slightest bit of added pressure before snapping.

Approaching the chaise, Cade stopped. He glanced from Lana to Esme then gestured faintly at the door.

"Give us a minute, ladies." However nicely phrased, his raw expression told the two women that he wasn't requesting their departure but demanding it.

They left quietly, their fingers whispering against Iris's arm as they passed. She felt their magic infuse her, little electric charges working to relax her muscles enough that Cade could steer her onto the chaise and wrap her in the blankets as if she were a doll he had to dress or an invalid who couldn't complete the task on her own.

He didn't speak, just leaned into her and wrapped his arms around her shoulders. Cade nuzzled her cheek and stroked her hair until she turned into him and hid against his chest, finally relaxed by the knowledge that her mate's presence would shield her from the worst of her memories.

A few more seconds passed, her energy growing calmer, and then the women re-entered. Lana took the position behind the chaise. The fine hair along the nape of Iris's neck rose with the uncomfortable memory of the metal gurney Oscar had been placed on and the Hunter who had held his head immobile while Quentin probed the cub's spine.

But Lana didn't touch her. The latent placed her hand on top of Cade's, her energy passing through Cade to Iris to be almost imperceptibly altered by his wolf and the alpha power he possessed.

"Thank you," Iris whispered to the latent, uncertain how Lana knew that touching her would have made things worse instead of better.

Gently capturing Iris's hand, Esme pushed more magic into the she-wolf. It layered on top of Iris's energy, sank into her bones and into her blood, where her heart circulated it through the rest of her body. She relaxed further, her mind sensing Esme's commands more than she heard them.

Slowly they worked through the final days that Iris could remember. Camille's visit, Hank's growing animosity after the witch's departure, the old man finding her tucked under a tree, her nose in a book.

A new detail emerged from those that had always chased Iris through her nightmares. Blood had stained Hank's shirt as he approached.

He spoke, the words unintelligible but something about Cade. He kept pulling at his crimson splattered shirt, his gaze wide with panic until she finally realized that Cade was hurt and Hank wanted her to go with him.

Her mind only half in the healing suite with Cade and the women, Iris told them what she saw, her voice as dull and lifeless as Hank's had been erratic and distressed.

Hank's behavior was a ruse, of course, but she sensed his trickery too late. Another wolf waited by his truck, someone she didn't know, so an outsider to the clan. She caught the flash at his open collar of a small pendant on a chain, both pieces made of silver.

"He reeks, like bad magic," she said. "And he's wearing silver jewelry."

She pawed the air, describing the pendant to Cade and the women. A claw mark, a wolf's scratch. The stranger's arm flashed in front of her, a fat streak of silver as he hit her hard in the temple with a heavy baton. She fell silent, unconscious in her memory.

And then she screamed, vibrations running through the carved walls of the healing suite as Iris found herself reliving the nightmare that had jolted her awake the morning of Oscar's interview.

There was a second wolf she didn't know. He had the same kind of necklace and pendant as the other man wore hanging from his neck. His stink clogged her nose just as badly. Hank forced one knee against her back to keep her pinned stomach first to the ground.

The first of the previously suppressed memories appeared. As Hank pinned Iris and clawed at her clothes, his pants were undone.

She tensed against Cade, her soft whimpers dotting the air while he wrapped his wolf protectively around her and Lana pushed more calming magic through him.

"You're doing great, baby," he whispered into her ear.

Iris felt love pouring from him, into her. Love, not disgust. His shirt grew wet beneath her tears, but he kept holding her, whispering encouragement as she pushed past Hank stabbing her in the chest, whatever plan he had in his half-dressed state unfulfilled.

Cade's wolf ran alongside Iris as she remembered her escape, her body shifting to her wolf form for the first time as she breached the clearing and heard the explosion. Somewhere behind her, Hank howled in pain and rage.

She kept running, her legs twitching along the ottoman in memory like a fox chasing a rabbit in its dreams. She followed Hank's scent and the reeking trail of the other men to a turnout on the side of the road. She knew the location from her few trips off clan lands.

A plain black sedan waited parked next to Hank's familiar truck.

The windows were down on Hank's old Ford, but Iris couldn't bring herself to approach it. She smashed one of the sedan's back passenger windows and rummaged for the key. She found it in the jacket shoved down on the floor.

Keeping one eye on the woods, she started the car and rolled down all the windows to hide the fact that one was smashed out. Hearing the infuriated snarl of a shifter, his feet pounding the forest floor as his arms broke low-hanging branches to clear his path, Iris peeled out of the turnout.

The back end of the car fishtailed from the sudden acceleration and loose gravel. The vehicle bounced over the low concrete divider that separated the parking area from the road.

Her head slammed against the driver's side window, the pain clamoring against the other agonies that tortured her healing flesh.

Pure instinct pushed her in the direction opposite the clan's lands. Only Cade and her grandmother would believe Iris. She had a long history of being something of an outcast among the wolves, her magic hidden so that she had less utility to the clan than the witches and healers who served them.

And Hank would make good on his threat, at least

with her grandmother. Even though he bore the same external good looks as his son, the man was pure ugly on the inside.

Better to let him think he had scared her away, or that she'd died from her injuries. Surely, she had left enough of her blood on the ground to make him doubt her survival. A few months and she could sneak back, find Cade and get her grandmother out.

A car passed on the road, the driver's shocked expression and the surprised jerk of his vehicle reminding Iris that her clothes were tattered and stained red.

Her attention divided between the rode ahead of her and the rearview mirror, she reached into the back of the vehicle and retrieved the jacket. Clumsily, she put it on, her mind turning over her future plans.

Could she really ask her grandmother and Cade to give up their entire lives for her? Her grandmother, maybe. She had been old when she birthed Iris's mother and Iris had been the only successful pregnancy in a long line of her mother's miscarriages.

Andra North had maybe a decade of life left and defending her strange granddaughter had made her almost as much of an outcast among the wolves as Iris was.

But Cade would be risking his life and giving up his other family and friends. She couldn't begin to understand his den instinct and what a hardship it would be for him to live away from the clan.

She wasn't a wolf, how could she?

Still dreaming the past, Iris felt Cade's arms tighten

around her in the healing suite. His voice rumbled in his throat, no words necessary to remind Iris that she was a wolf, had shifted in front of him the day before and during her escape from Hank. His fear reached into her memory, begging her not to forget her true form as she had once before.

*You are a wolf, love. My mate, baby. Come back to me.*

Iris squirmed in Cade's arms as she fought the urge to follow his energy back to the present. She had scratched just the surface of the lost time and needed to remember so much more, something that would help her, help the cubs and the two women guiding her over the rough terrain of a nightmarish past.

"I will," she promised in a whisper against his chest.

Her old self forgot about the shift, forgot about most of the attack, the other men, the way they reeked and the silver blade that had pierced her chest. She remembered only the threat of death if she returned—hers, Cade's, her grandmother's.

For two weeks, Iris moved farther from the clan, pawning everything of value that had been in the vehicle, stripping out the radio, and salvaging the tires and rims to sell them before she set the sedan on fire.

Hitching a ride with a trucker and going as far as a small town on the outskirts of Scranton, Iris kept only a small bag of the larger man's clothes and a lockbox.

It took another week before she opened the lockbox. She could have smashed it open before that, but the box carried the same smell of decay and rot as the two men who had helped Hank kidnap and almost kill her. Only desperation for more items to pawn had forced Iris to look inside.

She found more silver that she quickly sold, crystals and dowels that turned her stomach queasy but were worth a few bucks regardless, and a pile of papers with vivid pictures and writing in a language she couldn't read.

Some of the images were the wards she would later carve into her flesh, her mind subconsciously recognizing their purpose but the knowledge remaining buried until she had absently scratched one into her arm and the wound took a week to heal.

"What happened to the papers?" Esme asked, the question almost lost as it bounced and echoed from present to past.

"I had to leave them behind," Iris answered, the hidden thoughts and memories in her mind slowly resurfacing. "But I hid them."

Lana, the only one in the room who had experienced none of Iris's memories during the regression, shook her head in confusion. "But why leave them?"

"Simple." Iris pressed closer to Cade as she answered. Relief eased the burn in her tense muscles when he tightened his hold and kissed the corner of her jaw.

"Hunters found me," she whispered. "I just didn't know that's what they were."

# CHAPTER 24

S itting next to Cade in Denver's office, Iris listened in silence as those gathered dissected her memories. The only unfamiliar faces were Oram, the leader of the West Virginia clan, and Slater, the clan beta from Tennessee, his alpha too sick to travel and only tenuously maintaining power.

Other clan leaders were too far away. The decisions that had to be made about the care of the cubs could not await their arrival.

"You're saying Hunters have charms to pass as wolves," Oram started then jabbed a thick finger at Iris. "And only she can sense them?"

Esme waved her hand at his phrasing.

"There might be others who can smell certain kinds of magic *if they've ever been around it*, but Iris is the only wolf I've encountered. She also has other qualities that I've never seen in a wolf."

A little of the tension that had been building in Iris since the meeting convened eased. She had been worried Esme would start throwing around references to the All-Mother.

So far, so good.

"The two men assisting Hank were definitely charmed," Esme continued. "And, since Riya's death, I don't know of anyone other than Iris, wolf or witch, who can smell magic on someone. So, perhaps not the only one, but the only one living that we know of."

*Ah, damn it!*

The witch smiled, her magic pushing moral support in Iris's direction and, perhaps, an apology for bringing The Nakari into it.

Turning back to Oram, Esme adopted a professorial expression.

"There are two things we can draw from the shape of the silver pendants Iris remembers them wearing, and the conclusions are exclusive of one another in my opinion." She paused, waiting for Oram and Slater to indicate they followed her line of reasoning. "One is that a claw or wolf charm is used to control wolves. Forcing wolves who were strangers to Iris and not part of the West Virginia clan to assist Hank in trying to kill her."

Oram and Slater's brows knitted, much as Denver, Seth and Cade's had done when Esme presented her argument to them before the arrival of the two other wolves. Unfortunately, Oram had far less respect for Esme's intelligence. Iris felt that it would be a long meeting before the old wolf was convinced.

"The other, opposing, hypothesis," Esme continued, "is that the charm is used so that Hunters can pass as wolves. This hypothesis is bolstered, if not proven, by the artifacts Iris describes finding in the car. The two men, whether wolves or Hunters, acted as couriers for high-level Hunter material. While I believe that we can use some of the glyphs and incantations Iris has described to neutralize or extract the crystals from the cubs, I'm certain they were developed by Hunters. And why would wolves have them in their possession?"

"But this cub Oscar shifted and he supposedly stinks of the same magic!" Oram argued, his gaze skipping uncomfortably to Iris. "And you can't say it's because of the crystals...or does the head of the damn Witches' Council stink, too?"

Oram's question about Esme provoked a growl from Denver.

"I guess that depends on whether you like oranges," Iris answered before Denver could turn the meeting into a brawl. "Look, this is new. I haven't even been here a week—"

"No, you haven't," Slater said, finally opening his mouth to do something other than breathe.

The look Cade shot him had the Tennessee wolf trying to fade into the chair he sat in.

"And my exposure to magic for the last twelve years has been limited," Iris continued, her hand landing lightly on Cade's arm in the hope it would calm him. "When Esme or one of the witches is actively casting, I can catch a scent of it. But it doesn't linger on the object charmed. And Esme is casting basically every waking hour of her day to keep the clans safe. But, hey, if you all want to wait around a couple of days and have her do zero casting, we might learn that her magic is cancelling out the odor of the magic that put the crystals in her."

"Care to have your dicks hanging in the wind that long, guys?" Denver asked Oram and Slater.

Silence followed his question.

Iris felt the fine hairs on her arm lift in warning. With every encounter she'd had with the gingery wolf, she had made a careful study. Most of the time he seemed too relaxed, bored even. But she knew better. He was a deep thinker—and a consummate predator. When it came to disagreeing with Esme on anything, especially on removing the threat of the crystals, Oram was an adversary...prey, even. Far from bored, the wolf in Denver merely waited for the right moment to snap its jaws around the other man's neck.

It didn't take long—just another dismissive pass of Oram's hand when Esme tried to steer the conversation back to recovering the papers Iris had found.

Denver leaned forward, his hands resting lightly on the surface of his massive desk, and stared at Oram. The battle was silent and quick, wolf parrying with wolf, but Iris felt each blow exchanged. With the palpable tension running through everyone else in the room, they felt it, too.

Oram began to redden, the challenge from such a newly installed clan leader a high breach of wolf protocol.

But there was no protocol higher among the wolves than leadership by the strongest among them. Iris could only imagine a handful of shifters as strong as the witch's mate, and one of them had his hand curled around hers.

In the end, it was Cade who broke the silence, looking at Denver as he spoke. "I'll take my team and retrieve the papers."

The witch inhaled sharply, her surprise the only physical acknowledgment of what Cade had just done. He had broken from Oram, who was still his clan leader, as surely as if he had stood up, crossed the room and punched the old wolf in the face.

And he had dragged his team along with him.

Giving Cade's hand a little squeeze, Iris drew his attention to her. "Just remember that you get 'mate' when you rearrange 'team.'"

His lips parted and she knew an objection waited at the tip of his tongue. She silenced him with a smile and another squeeze. "I haven't told anyone exactly where I hid them. And having a half-witch, who just so happens to be a homicide detective, on your team will improve the chance of success."

The room's energy changed, the air pressure plummeting. Both Iris and Denver, their faces growing pale, looked at the cause—Esme.

"A witch and a half," she whispered, her hands and lips trembling. "I'm going with you."

"The hell you are." Rising from his chair, Denver closed the short distance between him and his mate. He pulled her up with a fierce tenderness. The dark glittering of his topaz gaze threatened to physically restrain her if she made any attempt to go on the mission.

Esme, her eyes misting like a fog rolling in from the sea, placed her palms against her mate's chest. She didn't push for release, just gently reminded him of the crystals in her. "Other than the cubs, who has the most to gain from retrieving the papers?"

"Then I'm going, too."

This time she did push, her head shaking violently as she rejected the idea. "You're too important to the clan."

"You're too important to me." He cinched Esme to him, his hands interlocking behind her back. "The clan means nothing."

Across the room, Oram squirmed uncomfortably in his chair. Iris looked at her hand as Cade gave it a discreet squeeze, the gesture and the push of his wolf telling Iris that Cade felt the same as Denver. His mate's safety came before the clan, before his status within it, before his very life.

Iris buried her face against Cade's neck as Esme slowly chipped at Denver's resistance.

"With the crystals in us, Oscar and I can't travel together any more than two cubs can." Standing on tiptoe, the witch nuzzled her mate's cheek. "And he needs you with him. You're the only father that cub will ever have."

"You're the only love I will ever have." Tears glittered in the big wolf's eyes, as if he had already lost his mate forever, her leaving only a formality. "You said we would always be together."

Esme slid her hand across his chest so that the palm centered over his heart as she answered. "And we will."

At that moment, Cade squeezed Iris's hand in return, the same promise echoing through Iris with the warm push of his wolf at hers.

# CHAPTER 25

"Why do we even think the papers will still be there?" a wolf named Remus asked with an hour's drive remaining on the run to Scranton.

Having already justified the belief that her hiding place remained safe to Denver and Oram, Iris ignored the big wolf riding shotgun next to Tanner.

Just four years older than Iris, she had known Remus since childhood. Like so many of the wolflings trying to impress their pack leaders back then, he had taken every opportunity to tell Iris she didn't belong. While his civility had improved over the last twelve years, he hadn't grown any friendlier or stopped despising her.

Not that she would have welcomed his friendship. Some bridges weren't worth mending.

"I'd like to know, too."

Iris glanced at the man sitting protectively close to Esme. The wolf, an early twenty-something male named Navarro, wasn't part of Cade's team. He served Denver, who had not yet chosen a beta to carry out his orders and lead the New York clan in his occasional absence.

Now, sent to protect Esme, his place at Denver's side was all but assured. Unless Navarro failed to bring the witch back unharmed, in which case Iris assumed the young wolf was as good as dead.

Cade glanced at his watch, then nuzzled her ear. "We've got an hour to go, baby."

She relented, for her mate and for Esme. The familiarity of the story would ease the witch's tension.

And, judging by the way the woman had her hands protectively wrapped around her stomach, Esme's anxiety bordered on unbearable.

"Before a second group of Hunters found me," Iris began. "I pawned everything from the car of the two who helped Hank—even parts of their car, like the radio, rims and tires. Then I burned what remained."

Navarro nodded, smiling at the idea that she had made good use of their enemies' property after killing two of them.

"The money didn't last long, despite my sleeping outside at night or only buying a single change of clothes and a backpack to carry them in at a Salvation Army for a grand total of six bucks and change."

She didn't explain the particulars of why the money

had evaporated so quickly. With her memory a blank on those weeks for a dozen years, she hadn't known herself. She had shifted for the first time during the attack by Hank and the Hunters.

She'd almost died from the injuries.

Her body needed fuel. Lots and lots of fuel. She had consumed as much food per day as she would have eaten during an entire week before the change. And it didn't stop her from losing weight. Nothing did until she had finished healing and subconsciously suppressed her wolf and its energy.

"It was raining, coming down hard, the wind so strong I could barely walk against it," Iris recounted. "I took shelter in a museum. It had been a school when first constructed and a stop on the underground railway..."

Sensing Navarro, and especially Remus, didn't want a human history lesson, Iris shrugged. "Anyway, I spent a couple of hours walking around it, waiting for the storm to die down. The place was loaded with silver—"

She stopped as a light shudder descended the younger wolf's body from his head to the tip of his steel-toed boots. He had mentioned taking a Hunter's spelled silver blade in his right thigh less than two months before during a mission to retrieve a latent.

The memory still uncomfortably pricked his flesh and made his balls shrivel.

"Of course, it was all behind glass so no one could steal it," she continued after giving him a second to recover from the memory. "But then I came up to this old desk that was only roped off and not all the way around. There were replica blotters and inkwells, a fancy letter opener that was fake, too, and copies of Abolitionist manifestoes and stuff—none of it real. But I could feel silver, just the faintest pull."

"Witches draw power from silver and iron," Esme explained as Navarro shot her a confused look. "We're basically metal detectors for those two elements."

Iris glanced at the front of the tactical van. Remus, who had prompted the discussion, appeared to be staring out the side window, but she could see his eyes in the reflection and they were fixed on her.

She turned her attention back to Navarro. "I figured there might be a hidden compartment, and I was right. Inside, I found a silver coin, very old. From before the Civil War."

The find had been both a blessing and her near destruction. Knowing its intrinsic value was far greater than any pawn shop would give her, she checked the phone book for a local antiques dealer who traded in coins.

Walking into his store, she had almost turned around and left. But she forced legs that wanted to run hard and fast in the opposite direction to approach the counter where the man waited.

She held her breath as the same stink that had clung to the Hunters who tried to kill her clogged her nose in that little shop. She convinced herself that the owner had merely, and quite innocently, acquired objects that carried some kind of magic with them.

She held on to that belief long enough to sell the coin for over three hundred dollars.

She had been wrong about the owner, of course, and the mistake almost cost Iris her life. She had returned to the diner she had eaten at the night before. She needed more fuel for her injured body and the manager had offered her a job.

With the money in her pocket and a kitchen full of food to borrow from, she would have enough money to last her until she received her first paycheck. That and the tips would carry her to the next paycheck and the one after that while she figured out what she needed to do to expose Hank Mercer and rejoin the only people who had ever loved or cared about her.

"So, all those years sitting around that museum and no one ever found the panel or whatever?" Navarro asked.

Smiling, she nodded.

"The guy I sold it to must have been a Hunter or at least known what I was." Which was odd, Iris thought, because, at the time, she hadn't known what she was. So how could he? "Anyway, less than an hour after I sold the coin, two teams of Hunters steamrolled into town. I had the papers on me and I didn't want to get caught with them, so I made my way back to the museum and hid them."

Satisfied, Navarro grunted. Young and overly charming, he leaned forward and offered her his closed fist for a light bump in appreciation of the clever wolfling she had once been.

She returned the gesture then relaxed against Cade. She didn't mention that a bus from a Poughkeepsie high school had shown up at the diner at the same time the Hunters appeared. She hadn't told Cade or anyone else yet about how she had followed the students back onto the bus.

Some of the kids had given her funny looks, but the terror in her eyes had silenced them. The terror and Jenna Barley.

Jenna was the school's cool outsider, a girl with a haunted gaze who lived with her grandparents because her stepfather had murdered her mother before committing suicide.

With one sharp glance, Jenna eliminated any chance her classmates would rat Iris out.

"What is it, baby?" Cade asked, his thumb discreetly stroking the inside of her wrist.

"Just remembering the girl who helped me escape...who then convinced her grandparents to give me a place to stay until I could get my own."

Cade blinked and his mouth turned down at the corners, a barely noticeable quiver dancing at the edges. Leading a mission that could be a cakewalk or a death trap, he didn't have the luxury of expressing his sadness for the time his mate had been alone and hunted.

But she saw it shining in his gaze and knew she would tell him later about Jenna and how, after everything Iris had learned since rejoining the shifters, she was almost certain the girl had been a latent. But she couldn't tell him at that moment. He had to focus on the team's safety and Iris would unravel if she thought about her lost friend.

"How close are we?" she asked, hoping to divert his attention.

Taking the tablet Navarro studied, Cade pulled up the location feed. Checking his watch, he growled toward the front of the vehicle. He returned the tablet to Navarro then scooted toward the back of the driver's seat.

"I don't care if it's past midnight," he snarled. "Slow the fuck down."

Tanner glanced in the mirror, his gaze landing first on Cade before locking on Iris. Her chest tightened and she shook her head, her gesture a warning or maybe a plea. Tanner had been quiet during the briefing, but nothing had suggested he wasn't focused on the mission. He'd gone through the checks as competently as Remus and Navarro, only without Navarro's banter and Remus's dour, back-handed remarks.

She hadn't thought anything about Tanner's silence, but she hadn't looked him in the eyes until that moment, fifteen minutes out of Scranton when they should have had more than half an hour to go. So she hadn't noticed the shadows haunting his gaze.

Apparently no one else had, either.

Iris thought of the source of those shadows—

Michelle. Lovely, young, fragile, broken—and genetically matched to a man old enough to be her father, a veteran who wore the scars of battle when other wolves remained whole.

Cade lowered his voice, his hand landing on Tanner's shoulder and squeezing. "I need you here, in this van, on this mission."

"I am," Tanner answered, his voice steady.

"You're not," Iris challenged, worried she was the only one who recognized exactly what was wrong. He already loved the latent, but he felt unworthy. Some ridiculous, chivalrous portion of him wanted to let her go, but he didn't know how. At least not directly, not while he was alive.

"He fucking said he's fine," Remus barked from the front passenger seat. He hadn't stopped facing the side window, but his eyes remained on Iris. "I don't care what you came back as, you're not in charge and you've got no fucking say. So let it go!"

Cade's hand closed around the big wolf's throat and applied an ever-increasing amount of pressure. Navarro jumped toward the front, his hand on Cade's arm and his lips less than an inch from the lead wolf's ear.

"Let go or we're turning around," Navarro insisted.

Cade glared at him from the side of one eye, his grip on his team member's throat tightening.

Navarro shook his head. "You may have lead on this, but I have final authority to abort. Let go or we're going home."

"It's too late," Esme whispered, hands still protectively clutching her stomach. Her skin had turned almost translucent except for two dark dots of red flushing her cheeks. She looked at Cade then Iris before explaining.

"We're not alone anymore."

# CHAPTER 26

"Not alone" was an understatement Cade thought as he low crawled along the rear exterior wall of the Lackawanna Founders' Museum.

Unable to turn back on the highway, he had pushed his team into Scranton, driving silently with the lights out through residential neighborhoods, looping slow circles, creeping along, parking for minutes at a time where they couldn't be seen.

Waiting for an enemy that never presented itself.

With only Esme sensing the presence of Hunters, Cade decided to proceed with the mission. He took Remus and Tanner into the museum, leaving Iris and Navarro in the van to protect the witch and act as lookout.

With a charm from Esme, the museum's security system was easily put out of commission. Locating the desk and secret panel, the papers still inside, proved even less challenging.

Everything was smooth as silk until they exited the building with Tanner running point.

A silver shrapnel grenade landed two feet in front of the team.

Cade knew he should be dead. Tanner, too. But they weren't because of Remus.

The man whose neck he had almost snapped earlier cast one apologetic glance over his shoulder then threw himself forward and down. The explosion lifted his body two feet off the ground before scattering it in pieces in a circle almost fifteen yards in diameter.

Witch light erupted a second later, missing Cade and Tanner but herding them away from the van where Navarro waited with the women. Cade dragged a stunned Tanner back into the museum, purposefully tripping the alarm system.

Cade figured in a town of less than a hundred-thousand people, in the pre-dawn hours, the police would be there in just a few minutes. That was all the time he had to reach the van, save his mate, and evade the cops.

But it was also all the time the Hunters had.

It took twenty seconds for Cade to reach the rear exit, five to push his wolf outside in search of the enemy, another second to open the door and pull Tanner with him, growling at the old wolf to keep his fucking head down because he did not have permission to die on Cade's mission.

*No one else was allowed to die unless they were Hunters.*

He and Tanner took another fifteen seconds to reach the end of the wall, two to hit the tree line, then another three before the van was fully in view.

Seeing the side door open, the interior pitch black, Cade's heart sank.

Then another bolt of witch light almost took his head off.

"There!" Tanner whispered urgently as he tapped Cade's right shoulder.

Turning his head, Cade saw a blue tactical van, three men and a woman sheltering behind it.

The woman was Camille Stone. And, if Cade had to guess, he would say the black-haired man beside her was Quentin. But no Navarro, no Esme, and no Iris.

The question of where his mate had disappeared to was answered a second later as twin blasts of opposing magic hit the blue van. Taking cover behind a heavy dumpster, Iris and Esme unleashed on their attackers.

Crouching next to the witch, Navarro aimed a high-powered rifle a few feet to the right of the van.

He fired. The bullet hit a fourth man previously unnoticed by Cade or Tanner as he returned from the direction of the museum. The back of the Hunter's head exploded, the momentum of the bullet forcing him backward where he fell into the bushes through which he had just low crawled.

Sirens pricked Cade's ears, their faint wail telling him

his team had maybe two minutes left. He pushed his wolf at Iris, capturing her attention.

He felt a flood of relief and joy burst from her.

His own relief was equally potent. Cautioning her back then, his hand did a small twirl with the index finger extended, focusing her thoughts on the sirens.

Next to him, Tanner started to crawl forward. Cade grabbed his collar. Tanner tried to shrug it off.

"Let me draw their fire," the older wolf pleaded.

"You will damn well hold position until I tell you to move!" Cade snarled, his grip on Tanner's shirt unrelenting. "Remus didn't die so you could turn around and commit suicide."

Cade gave another push of his wolf, this time at Navarro. The younger man's reaction was only slightly less exuberant than Iris's had been at discovering him alive. Cade grinned at the young shifter despite the dire circumstances.

Discreetly gesturing to Navarro that he should turn his rifle on the men hiding next to the blue van, Cade released his hold on Tanner.

"Go," he whispered.

Tanner moved forward. One of the Hunters, his gaze locked on Tanner, pulled a pin on another silver shrapnel grenade. He missed noticing the rifle pointed in his direction as he pulled away from the van to throw the grenade.

Navarro's bullet tore through his eye socket. The pin dropped from the dead man's hand and then the grenade fell next to it.

The explosion took out the Hunter standing next to him, nothing remaining of either man but meaty red splotches on the van and ground. Quentin staggered toward Camille. Blood seeped from his chest from the grenade's shrapnel.

Half falling, he lunged toward the old witch. His hands found the sides of her face. He yanked her close, his mouth opening, sucking at air until blue light flowed from the woman into his body and he started to heal.

Another bolt of magic erupted from the dumpster and then Esme ran toward her mother. Quentin hesitated a second, his mind calculating the chance of catching the young witch and draining her before escaping.

Another bullet from Navarro ricocheted off the vehicle, changing the man's mind.

Or maybe it was the sirens and the barely detectable flash of blue and red as the first police cruiser turned onto the street that made Quentin run. Cade didn't care. Tossing the bag with the papers to Tanner, he screamed for the rest of his team to get into their vehicle.

Not waiting to see if they obeyed, he raced toward Camille, hoping to intercept her before she could harm Esme or Iris. The woman raised her hand. The blue glow at the end of her fingertips told Cade that Quentin hadn't consumed all of the witch's magic.

He only hoped she didn't have enough left to fry his ass at such close distance.

Red fur flashed in front of him, and then three of

Camille's fingers disappeared down the throat of the loveliest, deadliest she-wolf he could ever imagine.

The van, with Navarro driving, screeched to a halt beside the old woman. Iris jumped in next to Esme and Tanner, turned swiftly and clamped her jaws on Camille's shoulder as Cade lifted the traitorous witch toward the van.

Cade slammed the van door shut.

Navarro hit the gas and what was left of the team got the hell out of Scranton.

# CHAPTER 27

Camille Stone sat bound to a wooden chair. Both hands were wrapped to keep her from spelling with them, her feet similarly restrained.

A ball gag filled her mouth, except when Mathis or Ta-Lynn, the witch he was paired with, expected Camille to answer a question.

Camille maintained her silence throughout.

She remained rigidly upright, her icy blue gaze alight with contempt for the interrogation team. For more than six hours, she had ignored all questions, no matter how civilly or brutally put.

The brutality did not come in the form of punches or kicks from the shifter, but from magic. For a few seconds at a time, Ta-Lynn would inflict an excruciating pain on Camille. The older witch's body seized, her veins and eyes bulged. Blood seeped from her pores.

Short breaks were taken to hose her off, and then another witch would appear to heal the damage inflicted. With the interrogation team back in the room and Camille's clothes still wet, Ta-Lynn would run electricity or ice through the material.

Burning, squeezing, freezing—the torture lasted for the span of a few heartbeats. Then came the questions, followed by silence, followed by more torture.

Iris watched the attempts on a live video feed, her back as stiff and straight as Camille's, her head occasionally moving side to side to express her disapproval of the methods used. It wasn't the violence that was getting to her, but the knowledge that the approach was pointless.

Torture didn't work against criminals, especially hardened ones like Camille, a woman who had invested everything in her relationship with another suspect.

Even when the prisoner broke—and everyone eventually broke—the information was most often unreliable. Any and all manners of lies were fabricated to stop the torture for even a few minutes.

The methodology also extracted a toll on the interrogators. Iris had intercepted Ta-Lynn in the restroom, the young witch throwing up in the toilet then standing in front of the mirror and spelling her face to remove the evidence of her tears and revulsion.

As a fresh round of abuse began, Cade sat next to Iris, her irritation ballooning and his wolf trying to persuade her against storming into the interrogation room.

"We don't know how powerful she is," Cade warned.

"Every failed spell to help the wolves was likely a charade. And it's no coincidence that my father had the help of Hunters disguised as wolves within a few weeks of her visiting you about the…well, the shifting issue. Her entire life with the clan has been a lie."

Iris's gaze flicked in his direction then back to the screen.

"The truth can't be tortured out of her," she said. "Camille won't crack that way. It's all about her ego and her relationship with Quentin. He was going to take her life and she still won't give him up. It's a combination of cultish behavior and what is likely decades of domestic abuse. She will forfeit her life, her daughter's life, whatever that psycho demands."

On screen, Mathis threw up his hands, looked at the camera, and shook his head.

"Can I go in now?" Iris asked.

Cade's head danced around, his firm lips shaping and discarding replies.

The choice was his. Denver, realizing he could not be objective, had made that clear. He had also banned his sweet, weeping wife from the holding area.

Rechecking the load on his 9mm pistol, Cade gave a curt nod and stood.

"Two things," Iris warned. "First, don't show surprise at anything said in there. Second, you're not going to threaten her with that."

"Baby," he said, pulling the door to the observation room shut once Iris was in the hall. "When I pull a gun, it's a promise to put a bullet in someone's head if they make a wrong move. It's never a threat."

She offered a soft growl of reprimand, her wolf pushing at him with the message that she was in charge of the interrogation.

Grinning, he handed her two small pieces of foam. Staring at them, she frowned then put a piece in each ear. His smile unflagging, Cade mirrored the process with another two ear plugs, and then he opened the door to the interrogation room.

"Take a break."

Mathis and Ta-Lynn filed out, Mathis casting one last menacing glare at Camille while Ta-Lynn's gentle brown gaze implored the older witch to finally relent.

"Now," Cade said, shutting the door once it was just him, Iris, and the prisoner in the room. "It's time to go over some new ground rules before Miss North talks to you."

"Rule number one…"

Grabbing the back of the wooden chair Camille was tied to, he jerked then dragged it until it was about one inch short of touching the room's stone wall. Taking aim with his pistol, he pulled the trigger and took out half of the right back leg.

He caught and balanced the chair, his unforgiving gaze on Camille's face. Fear and loathing narrowed her gaze and her thinned lips, which was more often than not fixed in a sharp, thin slash of contempt.

Moving around to the other side of the chair, he fired

again, then balanced Camille against the stone wall. The position forced her to bend her neck if she wanted to look at him or Iris.

"That was rule number two, in case you're keeping count, witch."

The entire time, Iris displayed no reaction to what Cade did. With his show of dominance over, she moved between Cade and the woman.

First, she checked Camille's ears. Seeing blood seeping from one, she healed it with a few words and carefully directed witch light.

Before moving away, she pulled the gag from Camille's mouth.

Cade's instant response was to place the tip of the 9mm against the witch's head and keep it there.

"You don't want to find out about rule number three," he growled.

"Do you remember me?" Iris asked Camille after his words stopped echoing in the room.

"Cade's bitch," she mumbled, then sneered, her lips twisting in a jagged line. "Andra's precious brat. Utterly worthless to everyone else."

"Well, I've managed to pick up a few skills since then," Iris said before lapsing into silence for a few minutes. "Anything you want me to tell your daughter?"

"I'll wait to tell her myself."

Iris dismissed the possibility with a twitch of her hand. "You think Esme's mate is letting her anywhere near you while she's carrying his cub?"

"Lying bitch," Camille snapped.

"*I'm* lying?" Iris laughed.

Camille's nose bobbed upward as she rolled her eyes.

Iris returned to stand in front of Camille.

Bending down, she pressed her forehead to the witch's and whispered. "It was too soon to smell it during the retrieval mission, but I thought you'd be interested to know that your daughter is *pregnant with Denver's child.*"

# CHAPTER 28

I ris let the words sink in before driving in a new barbed hook. "Esme is over the moon, of course. She won't risk the cub for your sorry ass. She knows you'd let Quentin kill her in a heartbeat...I mean, can you imagine the level of power inside her now that she's carrying a cub?"

Camille shook her head, eyes glaring, teeth grit as she hissed out, "You're still lying—bitch. And Quentin would never hurt her."

Iris's jaw dropped open. "So everyone's been lying to me about how Quentin broke her hands, strapped her to an altar and powered up some mad scientist crystal structure to drain her power for himself?" She scoffed. "That's a lot of bullshit for you to have swallowed for so long, Camille. You want a breath mint for that?"

The witch closed her eyes, her jaw working.

Worried that the woman was tonguing a spell, Iris

jammed her thumb into Camille's mouth and yanked her bottom jaw down.

"Look," Iris barked. "My mate has an itchy trigger finger. Don't give him an excuse."

She had to pause as Cade pushed his wolf at her, the energy so warm and sweet Iris felt like she might explode.

She reciprocated in kind, the sensation she sent him both a quick hug and a light, admonishing tap for interrupting her work flow.

Releasing Camille's jaw, Iris wiped her thumb on her pants, her face twisting in a grimace.

"I don't know why I'm wasting time talking to you, witch. The wolves have it right. You're just some rancid bitch who would sacrifice her child to…what, a lover? He seems too young for you."

Camille's eyes drifted shut. "He was born before your grandmother and before her mother. When our work together is finished, he'll have more than enough power to make me young—"

Iris snorted, the sound snapping Camille out of the reverie she'd fallen into.

"You really bought those magic beans," Iris laughed, her face pushed close to Camille's so that the woman had to look at her. "You mutilated your child when she was just a little baby, let him put the crystals inside her. You worked with the healer Gordon to have Esme kidnapped and her magic drained, and now, after he tried to drain you, you're still brainwashed. I bet you have a ready-made excuse for everything he's done, but it's all bullshit, babe. And I don't want to hear it."

Iris turned and walked toward the opposite wall, shaking her head as if she'd already given up on the witch telling her anything. Reaching the other side of the room, she leaned against the wall.

Camille had drifted into a trance of the addicted. Cocaine, alcohol, or an abusive lover—one cause was often indistinguishable from the other when they fell into that state, a beatific smile announcing they had reached their destination.

"The crystals are so we always know she is safe," Camille murmured. "He only took some of my magic so he could rescue us both, and why would he kill his own child? His firstborn…his little princess?"

Iris wanted to gag with every sentence that came out of the witch. With the energy rolling off Cade, she knew he felt the same way. But nothing could be allowed to interrupt Camille's flow.

Never shut a suspect up once they start talking. Wait for them to stop, then give them a prompt to see if you can restart the confession engine.

"Just how does that work?" Iris asked, her tone that of a fawning student in the presence of her favorite professor.

Arrogance lifted the right side of Camille's nose and the corner of the lip beneath it.

"Two witches fucking," she answered, her gaze rolling in Cade's direction before she returned her attention to

Iris. "I would have thought you understood the mechanics by now."

"Right." Iris's hand did a little dance of understanding. "That explains Esme's birth—but not her twin's. You remember her twin, right? The wolf he keeps tied down to a gurney, perpetually pregnant judging by the number of cubs the clan has rescued in the last six months."

For the first time since she had lost most of her fingers on one hand from Iris's bite, Camille looked shocked.

"Yeah," Iris poked. "We know about that. We know all about the piece of shit you keep protecting even after he tried to kill the daughter you claim you love."

Camille turned her head, her gaze scanning the room for the camera she knew had to be in there. With nothing but two other chairs and a wall clock, she stared at the clock as she spoke.

"We only took you to make sure you would be able to find the cubs, honey." Camille cooed. "It was all a charade to get the papers in your hands. Only that false friend Lana was in danger."

"Lie," Iris whispered, then repeated the word, her volume growing each time. "Lie, lie, lie."

"Tell me the real reason he put the crystals in Esme?" Iris said, her voice falling soft again. "He didn't put them along her spine like he did with the cubs."

Reaching down, Iris placed her open palms against Camille's lower stomach. She had been ready to make a point about the crystals working to make Esme infertile, but the words froze in her mouth.

"There are crystals in you, too."

Camille dipped her head. Her tongue looked, for a second, like Q might have spelled it from working if she started to reveal too much. Lips twisting like a possessed demon, the old witch pushed out a strangled grunt, but no words.

Camille blinked. The release of tears that came with the motion surprised Iris.

"It's to save us from birthing any monsters!"

Iris took a step back, stomach roiling as nausea made her dizzy.

Camille began to cry, but the tears of the guilty had never effected Iris. Her instincts, fueled by her magic and her wolf, had accelerated her career in the police force.

She was the youngest cop in Syracuse to make the rank of detective, and again when she joined the homicide squad. She had years of experience sitting across from someone who had killed a person they claimed to love. Infants, toddlers, teens, girlfriends and wives—victim after victim.

Every killer had a rationale, no matter how ridiculous, that absolved him or her in their own mind, that let them believe they had been a loving spouse, parent, or child.

"Wow, you're a crazy bitch," Iris said, grabbing the gag from where she had tossed it on the floor.

"You helped murder babies to put crystals in your daughter and the cubs."

Camille slowly swung her head from side to side. "No babies murdered, just cubs—"

Growling, Cade jammed the tip of his 9mm harder against the witch's head.

Iris pushed her wolf at him in warning.

*Control yourself or get the hell out of my interrogation room!*

Jaw clenched, he relaxed his grip on the weapon.

"You killed your own grandchildren to put crystals in the cubs," Iris continued.

Struggling against her bindings, Camille dismissed the accusation. "Don't think of it like that."

"You murdered your grandchildren. You let Quentin rip them from Esme's twin."

"No," Camille shook her head, a smug expression stretching her face. "That one is afterbirth, a placenta made to grow a head and a trunk with just enough of a brain to keep the blood flowing. I only have one child. There have been no grandchildren."

She paused, her expression growing more cruel as her gaze returned to the clock with its hidden camera.

"There never will be."

# CHAPTER 29

"Was she saying Oscar saw another golem when you were in his memories?" Cade asked Iris as they replayed the video of the interrogation to Esme and Denver. "But how could a golem birth anything, let alone cubs?"

Iris felt her last meal struggling to come up. It had been eggs and ham. It was about to become an omelet splattered all over the thick rug that covered the cave floor.

"Turn it off," she said, her hand brushing Cade's right before she robbed him of the remote and stopped the replay. "We can't believe anything she said, especially since she knew Esme would see this."

Silent for the whole of the replay, Esme chewed at her thumbnail as she continued staring at the screen that had gone blank. Denver waited a few more seconds before giving his mate a gentle nudge.

"What are you thinking, Ems?"

When she looked at him, her gaze was wet, but the tears remained unshed.

"I know you love her," Iris began.

Her words captured the witch's attention. Esme gave a little shrug followed by a shake of her head.

"My mother has lied for so long," she said, "she no longer knows what the truth is. But she can still be of use to us."

"Not as bait," Denver snorted. "Whatever she thinks her value to that bastard Quentin is, he won't risk a hair on his worthless ass to rescue her. In the meantime, we don't know what else those crystals inside her are capable of."

"That's the first thing she will help us with," Esme answered. "Even if it's just her being an experiment on how to take them out."

"Removing them could kill her," Iris warned.

"The Witches' Council has already discussed the risk. We find it acceptable." Her hand came up as Denver started to say something. "The clans can only banish her. It is up to the Council to mete out any other punishment for the breaking of her ancestor's oath."

"But she was freed from that oath," Denver said. "She fled before a new one could be extracted."

"Freed after the crimes were committed," Iris pointed out. "Unless that's some kind of loophole in the covenant."

"It's not," Esme said, her head tilting at a sound or disturbance only she could hear because the spell cloaking the room was hers. "Excuse me for a few minutes. Silantra has arrived and she seems very agitated."

Less than a minute passed before Esme burst back into the room.

"All of you, come with me. We need to move Camille now!"

"Tell me," Denver ordered, his tone descending into a growl. "Now, love."

She shook her head, her hands moving like small, nervous birds after spotting a hawk in their territory.

"She's spelling," was all the witch would say.

Cade shot a look at Iris. She shrugged, knowing as well as he did that they had left Camille bound and gagged with strict orders for her to remain that way.

"The only way is if someone freed her," Iris told him as they passed through the iron doors that led to the cavern's holding cells.

"Apparently not," Esme said. "She's humming…the resonance is…hot."

Before anyone could ask what she meant, they saw a red glow filling the room ahead of them. Esme rushed forward, her feet floating a few inches above the ground as a shield of witch light appeared in front of her.

His instinct to protect his mate overriding his duties to the clan, Cade reached for Iris. She surged ahead of him, flying as the witch did.

He rounded a corner, Denver keeping pace. Iris and Esme pushed past a line of shifters and witches, the group parting to reveal Camille at the center of the red glow.

Esme reached her mother first, the glow blending to purple. Her hands, nearly white with the intensity of magic flowing through them, pierced her mother's flesh, wrapped around the crystals and held fast.

Pained screams tore through Esme's throat as her mother stared passively. Iris braced Esme, healing her as the power surging within Camille burned Esme's flesh. Cade and Denver grabbed Iris, directed their power to flow into both women.

Purple receded to blue. Camille collapsed to the ground, dragging Esme and Iris with her.

"Open the last door," Esme rasped, her hand bloodied as she pointed down the hall.

Ta-Lynn and Navarro were the first to move. The young witch grabbed him by the wrist and started running. Mathis and Silantra picked up Camille's limp body as Cade and Denver helped their mates stand. The two women followed the others, hips and shoulders touching, a mate on each side.

"What is this?" Iris asked as they reached a massive door at the end of the hall.

"The door to the crystal chamber," Silantra answered in a monotone. "We shouldn't have come this way. We need to stake her down in the open…or execute her now."

Denver growled at the suggestion his mate had steered them wrong. Silantra tried to stare him down, failed and looked away.

"Only the All-Mother can open it," she explained, her tone hot as she jabbed a finger in the door's direction.

"And even Riya couldn't get the door to budge after she first fell sick. It's been closed more than a quarter century."

Reaching out from where she sheltered in her mate's arms, Esme cupped Iris's shoulder.

"Try it," she whispered.

Tongue swelling with a string of protests, Iris rolled her eyes. Then Camille groaned.

"What's behind the door?" she asked.

"Think of it as a super max unit," Esme answered. "I think my mother was about to go nuclear using the crystals inside her. But beyond that door, we can put her in a suspended state so I have time to find an answer."

Gasps and grumbles circled the group. Some sounded like they disbelieved Esme's claims, others—especially among the wolves gathered—sounded like they agreed with Silantra about putting a bullet in Camille.

Cade scanned their faces, his voice inflexible when he finally spoke.

"Putting a bullet in her doesn't end the war, just one battle with a bitter woman."

Denver nodded his agreement, his gaze going first to his mate, then to Iris.

"Well, witch-wolf," he challenged. "Aren't you even going to try?"

She shook her head, but her arm moved to gesture the others back. Looking at Esme, she cocked a brow.

"There are no words," Esme answered. "Just pull and use your magic to will it open."

Still shaking her head, Iris grabbed hold of the thick bar that served as a handle. She wrapped both hands around it, closed her eyes and started to tug, her wolf and her magic whispering through her mind.

*Open, open, open...*

*Open sesame!*

Nothing happened.

Of course, nothing happened. Whatever she was, Iris knew it wasn't what the sweet witch wanted her to be.

Growling, Iris dropped her head and tried again, willed it open with her wolf and her magic, willed it with her head and her heart and her hands.

Nothing.

A firm touch landed upon Iris's back. She thought for a moment it would be Cade, but the energy didn't belong to a wolf. Esme's magic curled around her own. Then a hot rush of power hit Iris as Cade and Denver added the strength of their wolves.

Slowly, the door budged.

What should have been dark on the other side was a nearly blinding light.

"That's enough," Esme shouted after another minute of all-out physical exertion. "The gap is enough to get us through."

Releasing Iris, she turned to Navarro and Ta-Lynn. Wrapping her hands against the sides of Camille's face, she started chanting and moving toward the opening. Supporting Camille's weight, Navarro and Ta-Lynn followed Esme into the chamber.

Together, they placed Camille on a solid slab of translucent crystal. With a nod, Esme ordered them out of the room. Light built within the chamber, everyone outside of it shielding their eyes.

Iris felt Denver try to move past her, she shifted her weight to block him, a growl rumbling in her chest in an effort to warn the foolhardy wolf back.

The light disappeared. Esme stumbled out. She leaned against Iris, hugging her back as she ordered her to push on the door.

"We must seal it quickly!"

When it was done, the witch collapsed.

# CHAPTER 30

"Are you saying Merlin, Merlin?" Cade asked as he and Iris finished putting away their clothes in their new living quarters. "I thought Merlin was a he."

Shaking her head, she gave him a light jab in the ribs with her elbow, then moved the suitcase off the bed.

"The events recorded in the human world were polluted by male historians, of course." Pausing, she playfully stuck out her tongue. "The sorcerer was a she. Her name was Meralyn, *not* Merlin. And she was one of the All-Mothers who lived during the Dark Ages."

"You know this from the artifact?" he asked, sneaking his hands onto her hips and attempting to steer her toward the bed.

"I know it from Esme," Iris corrected. "She gave me the artifact to try to read, laid hands on me when I couldn't pull anything out of it, then tried a Vulcan mind meld—"

Cade's rough laugh was wet enough to fleck a little spit on Iris's cheek.

"Gross," she laughed back, pushing him away to wipe her face on her sleeve. "Anyway, I couldn't unlock so much as a fart from the artifact. The story is interesting, though. I looked up the wiki on Merlin and it says one of his powers was shape-shifting. And, in some of the legends, Merlin was suspended in a crystal cave. So was All-Mother Meralyn after a sickness came over her and she lost her mind—but not her magic."

A shiver passed through Cade at the thought of an All-Mother's immense power being wielded by a damaged psyche. He shook off the sensation, then pulled Iris back into his arms.

"So, is the head of the Witches' Council done trying to crown you as The Nakari?" he asked, his quick fingers undoing the top button on her blouse before she realized his intent.

"I don't think so," she sighed as the next button surrendered to his touch. "She just got tuckered out and Denver made her take a nap. Hopefully a female cub with a caul will be born soon and I can just be, well, whatever the hell I am."

"Devastatingly sexy," Cade offered, his gaze hot as he maneuvered Iris to the edge of the bed.

She sat down, lifted her arms as he peeled off the blouse.

"Deliciously hot," he added, sinking to his knees to loosen the belt around her pants.

"Hold on there," Iris said, the nail of her index finger pushing lightly against the flesh at the top of his breastbone. "What did you and Denver discuss before he sent us packing for the night?"

He rolled his eyes.

"That ginger pain in the ass wants me to be his second."

Iris considered the proposal for a minute.

"If you wanted, you could be the clan leader back in West Virginia—or Tennessee."

His head bobbed in agreement.

"But…" she prodded.

"But we're taking the fight to the Hunters now," he answered. "And the battles will be led from this clan. Not to mention that, whatever deliciously hot, devastatingly sexy thing you turn out to be, you still need to learn from the witches. Need to teach them more than a few things, too."

Smiling, Iris retracted her hand, then braced both arms against the mattress as she lifted her hips. Cade dipped his head, then he offered a hungry growl as he stripped off her pants.

Cade looked up, his gaze glowing hot with the power of his wolf.

"I'm hungry, baby."

Studying him, the angle of his hips, the glowing eyes, and the way the wintergreen and pine of his scent had mellowed to fresh, wet grass, Iris bit at her bottom lip. She inhaled more deeply, her nipples hardening as he rose up and planted a hand on each side of her shoulders.

His gaze retreated even as he continued to hover above her.

"I'm sorry, love. If you're not ready..."

Iris snagged two of his belt loops with her fingers. She held him fast, her purple gaze looking up at him as a smile eased across her face.

"I will always be ready for you," she promised as she tugged his shirt from his jeans then slowly teased her wolf by unthreading Cade's belt from the loops.

He stopped her. Hands cupping her face, Cade coaxed Iris into meeting his gaze. "I love you."

Eyes drifting shut, she drew in a deep, emotional breath and replied softly, "I love you, too."

She sucked her bottom lip in, hesitating. He shushed her before she could signal any kind of retreat. With a slow burning caution, he straddled her then softly kissed each cheek. Each fall of his lips voiced a promise for their future.

"Together, we'll undo the damage the Hunters have done," he said.

She offered a small nod, but couldn't control the increasing pace of her breathing.

It wasn't the sexy kind of panting, either. It was a panic attack in the making.

His mouth slid to hover just above hers. Then his lips softly brushed hers as his hips settled between her thighs.

She felt the bulge of him, the hardness. His tongue slipped into her mouth, the gesture tender.

"You won't lose your independence, baby," he whispered against her ear.

The need to hyperventilate eased. Her chest expanded slowly, her nipples brushing against his chest to draw a needy groan from her she-wolf.

"Equals?" Iris managed to ask, holding a tight rein on the need to squirm against Cade.

Unsurprisingly, he had anticipated the fear tugging at her before she could name it herself. It wasn't the recently refreshed memory of Hank or all the violence she had witnessed in the last few days, beginning with the death of her closest human friend for the better half of the last decade.

It was twelve years of knowing, every single day, she couldn't count on anyone or anything other than her own strength to survive and now, quite suddenly, knowing she had to give up some of that absolute control to remain with the clan and, most importantly, with her mate.

"Everywhere but in here," Cade rasped, answering her question before biting lightly at the curve of her throat. He slipped his hand under the waistband of her panties to cup and squeeze her mound. "Not with this."

*Gladly*, she thought and pushed her hips upward to fill his palm more fully with her arousal. Slipping his fingers into her tight, wet pussy, a strangled groan fell past his lips.

"Damn, your body drives me so crazy, baby."

Straightening, Cade pulled the last of his belt through the end loop and let it drop to the floor. He thumbed open the button on his jeans, his hot gaze on Iris. Slowly, he pulled the zipper down to the base, and then he stopped.

*Tease!*

Iris squirmed, her plush bottom pushing down against the mattress then lifting as her thighs tensed. She bit at her bottom lip, denting it with the desire she felt for her mate.

"Baby, you haven't agreed with me yet," Cade coaxed as he tormented her by pushing his briefs down just enough for the head of his erection to breach the confines of the fabric, the tip bouncing forward for one pulsing second as if lasciviously winking its desire at her.

"Not here," she hastily agreed. "Here you have my total surrender...my submission."

Victory danced in the deep chocolate of his pupils. One hand planted on the mattress, with his jeans and underwear down past his hips, Cade pushed aside the gusset of her panties.

She squirmed. He lost his grip on the cloth. With a hungry growl, he ripped the fabric covering her wet pussy and tossed the material onto the floor. Cupping her bare mound, he squeezed again.

A flood of moisture released at the pressure and skin-on-skin contact. Cade kneaded her heated flesh, teasing her clit, pulling and tugging until she was panting, nearly thrashing, wild and uninhibited, beneath his touch.

Just as Iris was ready to climax, he stopped.

"Get rid of the bra, love."

She fumbled her way out of the contraption, her hips questing upward the entire time.

Cade leaned over her, pressed his muscular chest against her soft breasts. The thick head of his cock rubbed against her clit. He pushed forward, running the length of his shaft over that sensitive, swollen spine as his mouth claimed hers. Hips pivoted, the motion a relentless grinding as his tongue thrust past her lips.

His fingers skimmed along her sides to seize her nipples and pinch.

*Mercy...he knew just what to do to drive her crazy.*

"I'm going to leave you sore," he warned before he abandoned her mouth and scored the sensitive skin of her neck with his teeth. "But you'll heal, baby."

*Hell, yes, she would.*

Iris gasped from the slow, hard pull on her breasts. Her pussy clenched at the same time, muscle crowding muscle as her sex wept for him to fill it with the cock that still rubbed insistently at her trembling core.

His hands darted to her hips. Gripping them roughly, he pulled her ass to the absolute edge of the bed. He pushed her thighs farther apart, splaying her pussy open and forcing a downward tilt to her mound.

Forcing Iris to maintain the position in which he had placed her, Cade pushed his rigid, swollen cock downward. His knees dipped then straightened, the fat head of his erection thrusting into Iris.

She shuddered, groaning from how the tip of his big cock stretched her and the forward cant of her pelvis increased the inward pressure on her clit. His ass bobbed, the motion delivering tight rubs just inside her pussy. She grabbed his biceps. Her nails dug into the firm flesh as a full-body quiver ran through her. She screamed, not in pain, but at the overwhelming intensity of pleasure.

His hand twisted in the length of her hair to command full control of her head. He tilted it back, her neck hyper-extending to force her lips open. He invaded her mouth again, the hard thrusts of his tongue at odds with the little rolls and shallow pumps he made below.

Despite her promise of submission, Iris wrapped her fingers around his cock and desperately urged him to penetrate her more deeply. She wanted him in her, knotted, too swollen to retreat.

She stroked his shaft, her pulse accelerating wildly when she reached the point a few inches above the base where he had already knotted. She whimpered, knowing he would slowly feed the wide diameter into her sex, stretching her more than she could imagine, the tension stacking higher and higher until he was snugly locked in place.

Leaning forward, Cade grabbed her head with both hands. He straightened, bringing her with him, and then he fell forward. His weight carried them to the center of the mattress and pinned her beneath his massive body. His arms moved in a masterful blur as he hooked the underside of her thighs. Her bottom lifted from the mattress and then he cupped the crook of each knee and spread Iris as far as she could physically spread.

His gaze glowed hot enough to burn holes in her flesh. The heat licked at her nipples, every part of her on fire as Cade sank deeper.

She felt the top of his knot reach the entrance to her pussy as her wet, pulsing pussy drew him in one broad inch at a time.

Iris jerked, everything below the middle of her spine immobile with her climax. Just her pussy moved, coiling around him, squeezing, questing, fluttering until Cade threw his head back and howled his own release.

The primal sound unfroze Iris's body. She ground upward, milking his cock as the balloon swelled and jerked, fresh load after fresh load jetting into the tight space to soak her insides. He filled her until his cum and her juices escaped the seal their bodies had made, coating his heavy balls and her quivering thighs.

Spent, thoroughly claimed, the room around Iris spinning from her euphoria, she melted into the mattress. Cade dropped his head, his gaze caressing hers before his mouth found her throat and gently sucked while her last ebbing contractions played out.

Rolling to his side next to her, Cade cuddled her in close, his eyes soft as he gazed at her, his expression contemplative.

"I've never felt this before," he murmured, brushing his lips against her temple and tightening his arms around her. "Both grounded and tethered at the same time. Everything is just…uncomplicated when I'm with you, but somehow also profound. To be honest, I've never thought much beyond today or tomorrow until now. Until you."

She gazed at him and smiled, knowing exactly what her mate was trying to put into words.

"I love that we found our way back to each other, too," she whispered. With everything she'd seen in law enforcement over the years, she was all too aware that sometimes, two people could love each other, but sadly not love their life together. "Guess I'm saying I love you, and I love us." She chuckled. "Clearly, you said it better."

He growled, eyes hot as he pulled her on top of him. "Agree to disagree. I want to hear you say it again, mate —that you love me and us—while you're coming on my cock….and then at least a few times a day for the rest of our lives."

# EPILOGUE

Waking alone in bed, Cade ran his fingers through his hair and stretched out all his well-worked muscles.

Silk sheets slid across his skin, the smooth texture reminding him of his mate's body. He rolled to his side, reached out and touched the empty side of the mattress, some of Iris's heat still lingering.

He pulled her pillow to his face, inhaling her scent.

For a few seconds, he considered sleeping longer, but his cock was awake and growing bigger by the second.

"Baby?" he called out, swinging his legs off the side of the bed and planting his feet. He wiped the sleep from his eyes, wiggled a finger in each ear, then yawned.

The sound of running water filtered through his senses.

Wanting to be clean before getting down and dirty was

definitely a female thing. Just one of the many little quirks he loved about his mate. She was a blend of strength, sweetness, and endlessly entertaining sass.

And so damn sexy he basically lived with a constant hard-on whenever she was within scenting distance.

Suddenly, an image of Iris naked in the shower crowded his imagination, more blood filling his cock as he pictured her hands gliding over her lush flesh, a bar of soap in hand, her thighs parted—

"Fuck," he lurched forward, vision blurring with need. His hand landed on the door handle. He jerked the door open and entered the hallway.

Guided by scent and the tether between them that just grew stronger every day, he tracked her location.

*The hall bathroom, definitely.*

Over the weeks since they first began sharing their private living quarters, Iris had taken up the habit of using it instead of the one attached to their bedroom because she woke earlier than Cade most days.

He grinned as he remembered the way she'd tiptoed back into the room a few mornings back, freshly showered, hungrily gazing at him, but doing her damndest to be quiet so as not to wake him. He'd felt her eyes on him as vividly as if she were caressing his skin, stroking his cock.

Best way to wake up, bar none.

Really, it was silly that she went to such efforts to try and let him sleep in. He fucking loved being woken up by his mate.

Having her be the first thing he saw every morning, being able to feel her in his arms the moment his day started was quickly becoming an addiction.

And yes, the morning sex was of course fantastic. But it was more than that.

He loved how she'd mock-grumble cutely about needing to take another shower after he'd get her all disheveled and sweaty again. He'd then "make it up to her" by joining her in the second shower and giving her as many orgasms as it took for her to be near boneless when he'd bundle her up in a towel and carry her back to bed so they could snuggle and watch the sun come up.

As far as morning routines go, he couldn't think of a better one to look forward to for the rest of his life.

The fact that this was something he hadn't been *able* to picture as a possible future over the last twelve years just made it all the more meaningful. Theirs was a hard-fought happiness he would never take for granted.

"Did I wake you?" she whispered when she popped her head out to peer at him from behind the shower curtain, turning off the water while he closed the door behind him.

Cade pushed his wolf at her as he replied, "No. But you should've. Then instead of one shower together this morning, we could've had two."

She smiled, responding by pushing her wolf at him as well, her feminine energy feisty and teasing as it curled all around him.

For a she-wolf who'd been apart from him for all these years, she was a damn quick study when it came to figuring out ways to tempt him past sanity.

Hell, just yesterday, she'd tortured him with an early-morning blowjob that had resulted in them having to buy new sheets to replace the ones he'd shredded every time she brought him to the brink and then eased off.

Maddeningly sexy she-wolf.

"Woman," he warned as he felt her energy heat even more. "I'm already rock-hard."

Feeling another tail flick coming from her wolf had Cade stalking closer and jerking the curtain aside so he could look his fill of his gorgeous mate.

*Fuuuck.*

Water dripped from her naked body, and she made no move to cover herself up from his hot eyes.

In fact, she stood there with her hands on her hips as if outright daring him to make the first move.

He did.

Tantalizing droplets hung from her nipples that he simply couldn't ignore any longer. Leaning forward, Cade sucked one nipple into his mouth as he captured the opposite breast with his hand. He tugged her toward him, carefully helping her navigate over the thin lip of tile at the bottom of the shower.

Releasing her nipple with a pop, he tilted his chin toward the door he had shut behind him. A shiver ran through Iris, signaling that she knew exactly what he wanted.

What they both *needed.*

She pressed the flat of both forearms against the wood, then shimmied her ass backward until she collided with the thick jut of his cock.

To their right, the long vanity mirror reflected their naked bodies, Cade all hard planes and Iris all soft curves, her flesh slick with water.

With one hand on her ass to hold Iris steady, Cade slid the other between her legs.

Hot and wet for him. *Damn.* Groaning, he dropped to his knees and buried his face against her swollen folds. His tongue dove deep, pushing inside her sex, flicking around as his thumb and index finger toyed with her clit.

Iris jerked, whimpering as she began all but riding his face.

That is, up until he stopped out of the blue.

Startled at his abrupt halt, Iris cupped her hands around his jaw, her darkened eyes worriedly studying his as he ran his gaze over her from head to toe, making note of all the subtle changes in his mate's body.

"Cade?"

He didn't, couldn't answer her, the emotions running through him now simply too intense for words.

He blinked, his gaze softening as he stared at the mate he once thought he'd lost forever. The fierce, button-pushing, alpha-as-all-hell female who he knew he'd never spend a dull day with for as long as they both should live.

Truth be told, had he been human instead of shifter, he would've sworn he was one blink away from crying.

"What's wrong?" she asked quietly, sinking onto her knees next to him, her hands folding around his shoulders poised to shake an answer from him if that was what it took.

His mouth stretched into a smile. Then he chuckled. Hell, she was so damn prickly and perfect for him.

At the sound of his amusement, Iris noticeably relaxed before asking again, "What's wrong?"

Shaking his head, he brought one hand to rest against her stomach as he pressed his forehead to hers. "I love you, mate. I can't imagine my life without you."

She leaned up to brush a kiss against his lips. "I love you, too. Always have. And I don't want to even *try* imagining a life without you constantly driving me crazy."

Again, so damn perfect for him.

"And to answer your question, nothing's wrong, baby," he assured her as he spread his palms out to span her soft belly, feeling the small and precious energy now growing inside his mate.

When he'd first felt it, he thought it was simply wishful thinking. But then the tiny energy in her womb uncurled at his touch, seeming to sense and reach for him as well.

His chest tightened when he saw the wonder and happiness in her eyes as her hands joined his. "In fact, love, I don't think anything has ever been quite this right."

—THE END—

TURN THE PAGE

FOR AN EXCERPT FROM THE FINAL

BOOK IN THE SERIES!

## Book 3: Marked by Magic

*(AVAILABLE 09/17)*

**Thank you for reading & (*hopefully*) reviewing!**

I hope you enjoyed this story and will consider taking a quick minute to drop off a review at the eretailer where you purchased this book.

Every single review means so much. Truthfully, leaving a review is one of the best, most significant ways you can support us authors in our careers, and help our books find their way into more readers' hands.

♥

And before you go, don't forget to check out my other books!

Being an author truly has been just a dream come true for me so THANK YOU for making this a reality. Getting to craft stories and bring characters to life wouldn't be nearly as rewarding (or as much fun) without amazing readers like you.

xoxo

# A Peek at Marked by Magic
## Hunted Mates, Book 3 (Series Finale)

— EXCERPT—

Summoned to a meeting by his pack leader, Mitch Tanner sat at the great table that had once been rung round with clan leaders from across the country—sometimes the world—and their most powerful witches.

For all but the last decade, there had been an All-Mother, too. Now there was little more than lingering confusion and grief, the clans mourning all that had been lost and a looming defeat that seemed inevitable at times.

Hearing the chamber's heavy wooden doors creak, Tanner cocked his head. Before his wolf could sense who was on the other side trying to get in, Denver Gladwin bounded up from his chair.

There were only two people in existence who could make the clan leader move at the speed of light. One was

Esme, Denver's mate and the head of the Witches' Council. The other was Oscar, an orphaned cub the Gladwins had fostered up until a few rough weeks ago.

As with all the other recently discovered orphan cubs, the boy had been relocated to a safe house off clan lands. A small troop made up of wolves and well-trained latents guarded him.

It was the same for each cub they had relocated. None of the boys could be housed together because Hunters had attached crystals infused with dark magic to the boys' spines.

There was no consensus on why the Hunters had done that, but the split in opinions came down to either the cubs served as homing devices to penetrate the magic that cloaked the location of clan lands or they were bombs waiting to be activated.

Tanner didn't discount that both possibilities were true.

Denver threw open the doors and caught Esme just as her legs folded. Beyond her, Tanner could see the small retinue of witches and latents who were fighting around the clock to keep the woman alive.

He only vaguely understood what was wrong with Esme. Some sort of bad magic conjured by the Hunters. The magic was tied to a golem that looked like Esme. Her mother, Camille, had a hand in creating the monstrosity.

There was more conjecture flying around that Camille also had a hand in keeping the thing alive. Now the traitorous bitch was in a magic coma of sorts, her immobile body locked in a crystal chamber.

Speculations about Esme's health included the possibility that, without Camille, the golem was deteriorating, its existence somehow so intertwined with Esme that if one should die, so must the other.

Tanner knew he wasn't capable of tracking all the moving pieces. He was the kind of wolf who needed a specific target. He craved something he could shoot at or a throat he could sink his teeth into, throttling his target until death or compliance resulted.

"Something has happened at Himrod!" Esme rasped, her voice like two gravestones colliding.

Worse than the words was the haunted look in her tearful gaze. Whatever that something was, the witch had seen it.

Hearing the location, Tanner pushed through Esme's retinue until he stood mere inches from Denver. Not only was Oscar at Himrod, so was Michelle Ripley, the latent who was—but could never really be—Tanner's mate.

Still in Denver's embrace, Esme stiffened. Her entire body froze in a rigid arc as her eyes rolled up until just the whites showed.

Anyone from the meeting who could help Esme rushed forward. Silantra, the previous leader of the Witches' Council, and Iris North, a she-wolf who could wield magic, laid hands on Esme, magic flowing through their fingertips to infuse her with healing energy. Behind Iris stood her mate Cade Mercer, his hand on her back, his wolf's energy a sort of psychic battery that fueled Iris's magic.

The stiff curve of Esme's spine broke hard. She folded in Denver's arms like a crushed cardboard box. He placed her on the table, straightening her limbs then cradling her head with one powerful arm. His free hand stroked patiently at her cheek in an attempt to rouse her.

Remaining at the chamber's threshold, the witches and latents who had chased after Esme dropped to their knees in a circle and attempted to cast for any information on what was happening in Himrod.

To Tanner, it looked like each woman worked as a silo, but with all of them collectively sucking the magic from the room as everyone around Esme focused on reviving her.

"Stop!" Tanner growled, his finger pointing at the center of the circle the women had formed.

Half a dozen angry glares lifted in his direction. His hackles rose even as his balls retreated higher into his body. His wolf wasn't weak, but magic was magic and these women were among the strongest witches across the country.

A twitch of their nose could twist his balls in a knot.

"He's right," Silantra said, one hand gesturing for the women to leave. "Do that far away from her."

After the last woman retreated, Tanner pulled the doors shut and returned to the table.

Denver continued stroking his mate's cheek, his deep voice trying to penetrate whatever force or malady gripped her.

"Esme, love, what is it about Himrod?"

Tanner restlessly shifted his weight, one foot to the other, back again, forward once more, his wolf fighting the urge to race from the room, hop on his motorcycle and drive to the outpost. No thought of backup or a battle plan, no concern for the cub, wolves, or any of the latents save one.

Sweet Michelle, with her sad, forgiving gaze—the mate Tanner would not claim but would die to protect.

"Both wolves are dead," Esme softly groaned, her voice tightly wrapped with anguish. "Their hearts harvested."

"Baby," Denver started, then swallowed hard to seal the crack in his voice. "Do you mean Oscar, too?"

The tension coursing through those close to the witch multiplied until she weakly shook her head.

"I sense three latents moving away from Himrod in a vehicle," she answered with a ragged voice. "I can't see them, but it must be Tavi, Philia and Nadine, because Michelle is with Oscar. She's trying to cloak them both... she's both stronger than she thought herself to be and she is drawing on Oscar's wolf. I can see him, just barely, but not her."

Tanner wanted to get to the witch, but he'd have to peel Denver away from her, a task he'd never seen anyone manage to accomplish. Anyone who tried wound up bloodied or dead.

"Baby," Denver coaxed. "Are you sure you're seeing this in the now?"

"Some of it is now," she answered. "The wolf hearts

moving, the latent energy around them. That is all right now and faint. What drove me from my room were images being sent to me—the slaughter, Oscar and Michelle picking blueberries for dessert, then the two of them hiding by the lake, Hunters moving through the trees, their flashlights searching back and forth. I could only see that so clearly because of..."

She trailed off, her hand vaguely gesturing toward her stomach.

Tanner knew what she meant. It was impossible to keep a secret for long around wolves and witches. Shifters heard things even if they weren't trying to listen, and witches could see things they weren't trying to view. News had spread around the New York clan that, like the cubs, someone had placed crystals in Esme when she was young, maybe even at birth. Unlike the cubs, however, Esme's crystals weren't attached to her spine.

Hers had been purposefully placed against her ovaries.

At least that was the gossip around *Witch Mountain*, and her little hand gesture was enough to confirm it for Tanner.

The confirmation brought with it a sinking feeling in his gut. The vehicle she could feel in real time with the latents and wolf hearts meant there was no cub. That could mean Oscar was dead or badly injured and Michelle with him, her body in the same state as the cub's.

Tanner's fingers smoothed across his scarred cheek as Cade picked up a two-way radio and growled.

"We have to get rolling now. I'll see if we can contact the guards just in case it is a premonition."

Denver cupped both of Esme's cheeks with his big, strong hands. He pushed more of his wolf at her, hair sprouting along his exposed skin and his body beginning to glow with the same topaz hue that lit his gaze.

"Baby, please, try to see Oscar," he pleaded as Cade moved into the hall with the radio.

Her hands moved down to her stomach, the dainty fingers and palms cradling her sides. "He…he's shivering…so cold and frightened. Water, darkness, his chest hurting and then moonlight."

She drew a deep breath. The jerk that came with the intake of air caused fresh tears to spill down her cheeks. "The hearts are with the latents. I can track them, but I have to get closer—"

Denver shook his head. As much as Denver loved the cub, as much a duty as he owed to the captured latents and the dead shifters who had sacrificed their lives, Tanner knew the man didn't want to risk his already sick, and slowly dying mate…

— End of Excerpt —

*Available at all eretailers Sept 17, 2021*

# WANT MORE HOT SHIFTERS?

*Check out my MC shifters series!*

PROTECTED BY THE PACK

Book 1: **Harboring His Mate** (*Taron & Onyx*)

Book 2: **Resisting His Mate** (*Braeden & Paisley*)

Book 3: **Enticing His Mate** (*Joshua & Clover*)

# About the Author

*New York Times* and *USA Today* bestselling author Christa Wick has been hybrid publishing since 2012 (yep, she's one of the O.G. indie authors). She's written 50+ romances starring curvalicious heroines and alphalicious heroes whose stories span the spectrum of: steamy & sweet, steamy & emotional, steamy & suspenseful, steamy & paranormal, steamy & dark, and...well, you get the idea. She also writes sci-fi thrillers and suspense novels under other pen names.

## New Release & Sale Alerts
→ *bit.ly/ChristaWickEmailList*

## Where to find me & my books:
→ www.christawick.com
→ facebook.com/christawickbooks
→ books2read.com/ap/n6dD7x/Christa-Wick
→ bookbub.com/authors/christa-wick